Give feedback on the book at:
lorhainneeckhart.le@gmail.com

Twitter: @LEckhart
Facebook: AuthorLorhainneEckhart

Printed in the U.S.A

A Vow of Love

A FRIESSEN FAMILY CHRISTMAS

THE FRIESSENS: A NEW BEGINNING
BOOK FOUR

LORHAINNE ECKHART

The Friessen Family Series
Reading order:

The Outsider Series

The Forgotten Child
A Baby And A Wedding
Fallen Hero
The Awakening
Secrets
Runaway
Overdue
The Unexpected Storm
The Wedding

The Friessens: A New Beginning

The Deadline
The Price to Love
A Different Kind of Love
A Vow of Love, A Friessen Family Christmas

The Friessens

The Reunion
The Bloodline
The Promise
The Business Plan
The Decision
First Love
Family First
Leave the Light On
In the Moment
In the Family: A Friessen Family Christmas
In the Silence
In the Stars
In the Charm
Unexpected Consequences
It Was Always You
The First Time I Saw You
Welcome to My Arms
Welcome to Boston (A Paige & Morgan Short Story)
I'll Always Love You
Ground Rules
A Reason to Breathe
You Are My Everything
Anything For You
The Homecoming includes When They Were Young
Stay Away From My Daughter
The Bad Boy
A Place of Our Own
The Visitor
All About Devon
Long Past Dawn
How to Heal a Heart
Keep Me In Your Heart

The Friessen Family

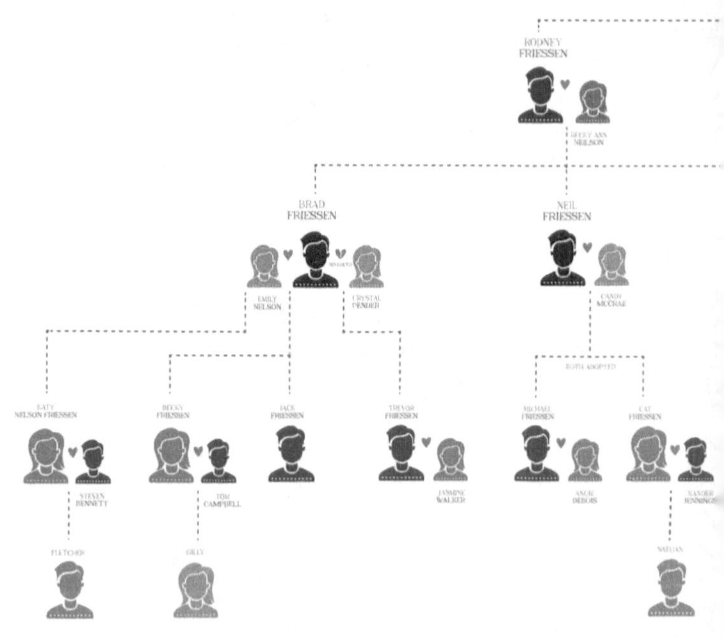

<table>
<tr><td colspan="2">

The Outsider Series

</td><td colspan="2">

The Outsider Series

</td><td colspan="2">

The Friessens:
A New Beginning

</td></tr>
<tr>
<td>THE FORGOTTEN CHILD</td><td>BRAD & EMILY</td>
<td>SECRETS</td><td>DIANA & JED with the entire Friessen Family</td>
<td>THE DEADLINE</td><td>ANDY & LAURA</td>
</tr>
<tr>
<td>A BABY AND A WEDDING</td><td>BRAD & EMILY & and Jed, Neil, Rodney, & Emily</td>
<td>RUNAWAY</td><td>ANDY & LAURA</td>
<td>THE PRICE TO LOVE</td><td>NEIL & CANDY</td>
</tr>
<tr>
<td>FALLEN HERO</td><td>JED, DIANA & ANDY</td>
<td>OVERDUE</td><td>JED & DIANA</td>
<td>A DIFFERENT KIND OF LOVE</td><td>BRAD & EMILY</td>
</tr>
<tr>
<td>THE SEARCH</td><td>JED, DIANA & ANDY</td>
<td>THE UNEXPECTED STORM</td><td>NEIL & CANDY</td>
<td>A VOW OF LOVE</td><td>THE ENTIRE</td>
</tr>
<tr>
<td>THE AWAKENING</td><td>ANDY & LAURA</td>
<td>THE WEDDING</td><td>NEIL & CANDY and the entire Friessen Family</td>
<td>A FRIESSEN FAMILY CHRISTMAS</td><td>FRIESSEN FAMILY</td>
</tr>
</table>

The Friessens

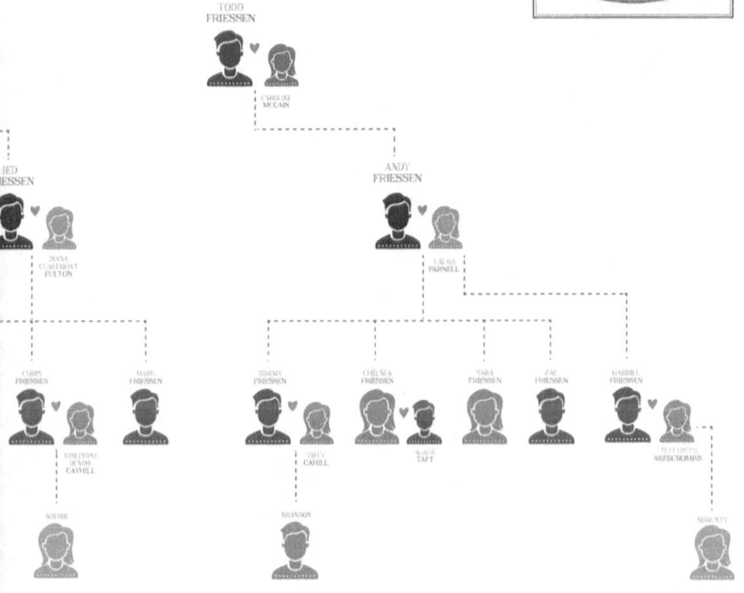

TODD FRIESSEN
CAROLINE MCCAIN
JED FRIESSEN
DIANA CLAREMONT FULTON
ANDY FRIESSEN
LAURA PARNELL
CHRIS FRIESSEN
JOSEPHINE DENISE CAYHILL
MARK FRIESSEN
JEREMY FRIESSEN
TIFFY CAHILL
CHELSEA FRIESSEN
ISAIAH TAFT
SARA FRIESSEN
ZAC FRIESSEN
GABRIEL FRIESSEN
ELIZABETH ABERCROMBIE
SOFHIE
BRANDON
SHAUNTY

—"Absolutely brilliant. Got my coffee, said to hell with the house-work, and devoured it slowly. I was gobsmacked at Rodney's story. Poor Becky. This family series is a bloody good read. Thank you."

—"Compelling, emotions run high throughout this story."

BOOKZILLA

—"Neil and Candy have had a dynamic relationship with a lot of passion and disappointments. Can true love and a renewed trust get them their happy ever after?"

J. MURPHY

—"Loved this so much! Neil and Candy have such a special love that has touched me and even more so now. This book is a must read!"

SUSAN

—"I read this book in less than 24 hours on my vacation with my husband and two year old. I couldn't put it down, I have already fallen in love with Becky and had to see what happened with Maria. Loved it."

AMANDA

—"The Friessen family is a family that really touches my heart and they will touch yours heart too."

Sometimes families need a helping hand

Holidays are about family, love, and giving, but this Christmas, the Friessens are in for a rough holiday season.

Thirteen days before Christmas, a letter arrives that Candy Friessen was never meant to see. When she opens it, she discovers a lie that rocks her world, and she begins to question everything she and Neil have created together, including his love for her and their family.

Seven days before Christmas, her heart breaking, Candy considers leaving her husband for good, and she begins making plans—until a call one night alerts all the Friessens that Becky, their mother, is in the hospital, fighting for her life. Without a second thought, the entire Friessen clan is on a plane to her bedside. Faced with uncertainty, Brad, Neil, Jed, and their wives are together for Christmas, but there's no happy celebration, no gifts piled under the tree.

For Candy and Neil, once trust is destroyed, can their family bond be strong enough to save their marriage?

Chapter 1

Would she ever get used to this cold, damp weather? Candy pulled at the collar of her thick wool sweater and rubbed her arms as a chill went through her. She pulled back the curtains and took in the steady drizzle of rain over the brown fields, which she supposed would be green come spring. These were fields Neil had promised to fence in, where her horse and donkey could one day graze. As she took in the heavy blanket of clouds that filled the sky, turning it a dreary gray, she wondered how long it would take her horse and donkey to acclimatize. After the hot days of Cancun, Mexico, life in the Pacific Northwest would be a rude shock, she was sure. Would they miss the sun as she did? It had been so long since she'd seen it. After endless days of rain, she missed the brightness of it against the crystal blue ocean, the warmth, and her animals. Even though this property was oceanfront, it was darker, different—colder.

Neil had been on the phone, making arrangements to close up their Arizona apartment and to have everything shipped to their new home, an acreage outside Hoquiam,

Washington, in the Pacific Northwest. It was close to Brad and Emily and to the family home where Neil had grown up. This was a new beginning for them and their children, and she never questioned his need for a fresh start. She could leave everything behind, except for her horse, Sable, and her donkey, Ambrose, whom she'd rescued as a newborn after his mother was killed on the side of the road. She still couldn't believe all the hoops Neil had to jump through to move her animals up here. Passports for animals? She'd never heard of such a thing, and Neil was just ending his call with a customs broker, compiling all the paperwork that was involved.

"Candy, didn't you hear me call you?" Neil was standing in the middle of their sparse living room. It was finished in light woods and currently held a lone black easy chair, which was the only furniture they had. It had been brought over by Neil's brother Brad to tide them over until their furniture arrived. They could have stayed with Brad and Emily, but Neil insisted after purchasing this house that they all needed space, they needed their own home. Not for the first time, Candy disagreed, but she said nothing. There was something about Neil: Once he set his mind to something, no one could change it. She sensed this was more about his needs, as there was a tension she couldn't put her finger on between him and his brother.

"Sorry," she replied. She swallowed as she watched Neil, his dark hair a little on the longish side, touching the top of his ears with a natural wave she hadn't seen when he kept his hair short. Threads of gray were now woven through his thick hair—even more this morning, as if it had happened overnight.

"The kids asleep?" He glanced at the carpeted stairs and the open railing leading to the second floor.

"Cat's sleeping in our bed," Candy said, referring to an

air mattress on the floor. Their new bed, along with a kitchen table, a living room suite, and a bed for Cat, would be here Friday. Just two more nights of rambling through an empty house. "Michael's only been quiet a few moments," she continued. "I hope he's sleeping. He's been so fussy lately. He didn't sleep much last night." At least he was sleeping in his own bed, a crib, the one given to them by Brad and Emily.

Neil didn't say anything about the baby. If it had been Cat having trouble, he probably would've gone to check on her. The difference wasn't lost on Candy. He seemed so distracted as he glanced down at the paper he was holding. "The broker needs papers on Sable—registration, birth date. Since there aren't any, I need to at least know where you purchased him so that I can trace the paperwork. Ambrose, since you had him from birth and found him abandoned, is a little trickier …"

She had her back to Neil and parted the sheers again, looking out at the steady rain. The day was so gray and depressing. Maybe it was the lingering silence that made her realize Neil was no longer talking. When she faced him, he was watching her in that way he had when he was trying to get into her head.

"What's wrong?" he said. He knew her too well, and sometimes she supposed that wasn't a good thing. There were times she needed space, but Neil wasn't a man who would give it to her.

"Tired is all, and cold." She shivered again.

Neil, too, was wearing a thick dark blue sweater and faded jeans. "We're just not acclimatized yet. You'll get used to it." He glanced at the fireplace. "A fire will help cut through the dampness. I'll call Brad later, get some wood from him." He went over to the wall, plain white, and touched the thermostat. "I can turn up the heat, but it's already as high as it should be."

"No, it's fine. It'll get too warm upstairs. Neil, even if there was paperwork for Sable, everything would have been lost in the storm. He was a gift from my dad. I don't know where he purchased him. Is that a problem?" She hoped it wasn't. Worry nagged at her. Would she ever see her horse and donkey again?

Neil started toward her and touched her arm, sliding his large hand over her shoulder and caressing her. He was so close, and she loved when he touched her like this. He didn't need to say anything to let her know how he felt about her. Their love was strong, and this bond between them … she knew deep in her soul that it was unbreakable. They'd been tested by things other couples hadn't, and she believed that had made them stronger, more connected. Nothing could ever come between them. "Neil, am I going to get Sable and Ambrose back?"

"Of course." The way he said it, she believed him. But then, Neil had this way about him. When he put his mind to something, he could move mountains. At the same time, she believed he'd do anything for her now. "I'll just have to be creative, is all. Don't worry about it. I'll find a way."

"Are you still planning on leaving Monday? What if you can't get the paperwork together, what then?"

Neil rubbed her arm, touching her still. He was right in her space, taking over as he always did, trying to fix everything for her. He ran his hand under her chin, and she had to look up. He was so tall. So was she, but he was amazing. Strength oozed from him. "I'll have it together," he said. "Don't worry. The guy I hired is good. Don't lose faith in me."

She had to hide her smile. Did he have no idea of how she believed in him? He was her hero, a man she looked up to, with all his flaws and bossiness. She truly believed that after finding their way back together, they wouldn't allow anything to come between them again. Neil had done that once, and it had almost destroyed her, but she could see his regret and feel his determination. It was unsettling but comforting to know she was loved so much.

"Are we ever going back to Cancun?" she asked. It wasn't that she wanted to go back. Cancun was filled with memories of hurt and betrayal—memories of the surrogate who had almost destroyed what Neil and Candy had.

Neil's expression darkened. "No, it's time for a new life here. We're done in Mexico."

She nodded. Maybe that was what she needed to hear, just a confirmation. At times, though, she couldn't shake the sense that they were hiding from something. "What about the resort, Neil? You haven't talked about it lately. Don't you need to be there to run the day-to-day operations? I know this was a really big deal for you."

The resort was being built on the oceanfront property that had once been hers. After a storm destroyed her home and she lost the land to her creditors, Neil had bought it and given it back to her. She had believed she couldn't live without it, but she was wrong. Her family was more important, and her life with Neil.

"I wanted to talk to you about that," he said. "It may be time to sell."

Was he serious? She had never seen him look so disinterested. After all the years of wanting that property, obsessing about building his resort—a resort that had been the biggest obstacle between them— he wanted to walk away now?

"I don't understand, Neil," she said. "Why would you sell it? You promised me a part of the beachfront would always be mine. You know how much it means to me."

"I won't sell if you don't want me to, Candy, but I don't see a reason to keep it. Our life is here now. Think about it. I don't plan on going back. We need to cut ties, sell, and move on with our lives."

She could hear Michael whimpering from upstairs. She sighed, and maybe it came out sounding uneasy, but she hadn't meant it to. She loved her baby, their baby, the little boy they'd adopted, but she was so tired. Michael had been more and more demanding as of late. "I'd better get him," she said.

She knew he wouldn't wake Cat, their deaf little girl, whom she'd found in a Mexican orphanage. Cat was such an inspiration to Candy, and she loved watching Neil with her, fussing over her, talking to her, reading to her when her cochlear implant was on. He did everything he could for a little girl he had wanted nothing to do with in the beginning. On the other hand, she'd yet to see him fuss over Michael, their baby, which was disconcerting. Maybe from the way Neil appeared distracted, not glancing at the stairs, she knew he wouldn't go up—not for Michael. For Cat, he'd already be taking the stairs two at a time. She should talk to him about it and make him listen this time, make him tell her why he was so distant when he'd been the one so obsessed with the idea of having a baby.

He waved the paper in the air. "I need to make some more calls," he said, then he left the empty living room through the kitchen, the floor creaking under his heavy footsteps to the small office at the back of the house, which still held a desk left by the prior owners. It was made of solid wood, old, probably something even Goodwill wouldn't want.

"Coming, baby," Candy called out as if that would reassure Michael, and she started up the stairs just as he let out a wail.

Chapter 2

It was the first time she'd been warm in days. She leaned back against the rim of the bathtub, her hair clipped up. Steam rose in the chilly bathroom, and she wanted to close her eyes for a moment as she listened to the quiet in the house. Neil was still here, and he always gave her a sense of wellbeing, as if he was looking after things. Tomorrow would come soon enough, when he had to leave. Her heart sank at the thought.

"You're not going to fall asleep, are you?" Neil was looking down, taking in all of her. She hadn't bothered with bubbles, and she could tell by the heat in his eyes that he appreciated the view.

"Cat asleep?" she asked, as Neil had been reading her a story when she climbed in the bathtub.

"Fast asleep in her own bed."

Candy was happy. All the furniture had arrived, filling every empty room. She couldn't wait to sleep on her pillowtop mattress, and it was nice to have their clothes in drawers, a dining table, a sofa. Neil had spared no expense.

She could do with very little, but Neil liked nice things.

"So, how about if I wash your back?" Neil pulled off his sweater and dumped it on the floor, then stepped out of his jeans. "And your front."

She scooted forward and let him climb in the bath behind her. She leaned back against all his hardness and his warmth. His hand went over her breast and then in the water, over her flat stomach and lower. He leaned down and kissed her neck, at the same time touching her where she truly belonged to him. He knew just how to caress her to have her spreading wider, as wide as she could in the confines of the bathtub. He ran his teeth over the skin on her shoulder, and she gave him more of her neck. He made her feel desired.

"Oh, Neil, do you have the baby monitor?" she asked. She felt him still, and she started to sit up when he flattened his hand on her stomach and pulled her back against him.

"The monitor's on the counter," he said. "Stop worrying. Now, where were we?"

Candy put her hands on his legs and turned. He must have had some idea what she was planning, as he put his hands on her hips and lifted her so she could straddle him. She could feel how ready he was as she ran her hand over his chest and through the dark hair that covered it. She loved to feel his pecs and lower, over his washboard abs. She didn't know when he found the time to work out, but she knew he believed it was important to stay in shape, not only to look good but to feel good. He said it kept the mind sharp, too. Right now, her hands appreciated the feel of his dedication to his body.

He slid his hand over her hips and started to lift her, pushing his way inside her, lowering her down and holding her until he filled her. She gasped as he ran one hand up her back, his fingers in her hair, pulling until the clip slipped out. He pulled her head closer. She could feel his warm breath as he parted his lips, and her eyes went to the fullness of his mouth, which could touch her and do things to her that drove her wild. She kissed him, his tongue touching hers. Even though she was on top, he was moving her, holding her, controlling her. He just wasn't a man to give that up, and she smiled against his lips.

"Hmm," she murmured.

He broke the kiss, his lips so close to hers. "What's so amusing?" He kissed her again, and she leaned into the kiss.

"You're not letting me have my way with you," she whispered back, feeling his warm breath. She could taste him on her as he ran his hands up her back, skimming her sides, touching all of her as a sly grin spread over his face. His eyes were teasing, at the same time turning a darker shade of brown. They brightened as he sank deeper into her, holding her to him.

"I love you, Candy."

She loved hearing him say those words, they meant so much more as of late. Now, with him buried in her so deeply, she could feel how much he meant it. It was in his touch, something he couldn't hide, not from her. Never like this.

He let her move.

"I'LL BE GONE ten days, and then I'll be home. We'll get a Christmas tree just like we talked about, and there'll be lots of presents underneath for you," Neil said, tucking Cat's shoulder-length dark hair behind her ears. It was so fine, just like a baby's. She stared up at him with such love in her light blue eyes. He knew she didn't understand Christmas. She'd never had one, being an orphan, stuck in her silent world. This year, he wanted to give her everything and see the wonder in her eyes when they first lit up the Christmas tree, when she saw the pile of gifts and tore open the shiny wrapping.

"Daddy, stay," Cat said in a flat voice. She was doing so well with her speech, and her cochlear implant was now attached behind her ear. She'd come so far, and he'd do anything for her—a little girl who was now his.

"I can't, honey. Daddy has to go and get Mommy's horse and donkey and clean out the apartment and our house in Mexico. I'll bring back all your toys." He rubbed her head and kissed her cheek as he held her in his lap. She fisted her hands in his sweater and wouldn't let go.

Candy was holding Michael, swaying with him in her arms, and he was jamming his fist in his mouth, fussing. "Michael, come on. What's wrong, baby?" she whispered, and Neil could see how tense she was. He could hear the frustration in Candy's voice, which was unusual, but then, Michael had been oddly fussy for weeks.

"Has he got a fever?" Neil asked, and Candy's lips firmed. She touched his forehead with her cheek.

"He's a little warm, but not overly. I'll take his temperature, but I think his tummy is upset. He threw up all his formula this morning. He has a few times this week. Maybe it's time I take him to a pediatrician. Emily gave me the name of hers. We need to have someone local, anyway, for Cat, as well."

Neil took in his baby, who was wearing a green striped sleeper, wiggling in Candy's arms. He could see how unsettled he was. He tightened his hold around Cat, and then all of a sudden, Candy started crying, tears streaming down her face. He stood, Cat in his arms.

"Mommy sad," she squeaked.

"Hey, what's going on?" Neil said. He touched her shoulder and slid his arm around her as she tried to rock Michael. Neil took in his baby's scrunched-up face.

"I'm just so tired. I don't understand why you won't hold him, Neil. Is there something wrong with him?"

When she looked up at him, he was taken aback by the misery he saw in her eyes. She was truly distressed, and it was obviously something she'd been holding on to for a while. "No, nothing's wrong with him," he said. "Don't create something out of nothing. You're his mother. I'm sorry. Why don't you let me hold him, and you can take a nap?"

"You have to leave, remember?" she snapped as she pulled a light blanket around the baby.

Neil put Cat down and was at Candy's side before he could think it through. He took the baby from her. "There's time still. Brad's not here yet, and my flight doesn't leave for two hours."

She gave him one of those looks, as if she didn't believe him, and he kept his expression together even though holding Michael and feeling the heat from his little body—his biological son—was tearing him up inside. But he knew how to hide what he was thinking, what he was feeling, and right now he needed to get his wife out of this room before she started asking any questions. She was figuring a lot of things out, and he didn't want to go down that road. He needed to pull it together.

"Are you sure?" She hesitated before tucking long strands of hair behind her ears, then watched him. No, it was more like studied him. He wondered if she was about to say something as Michael started fussing again and wiggling in his arms.

He had to look down at him. Taking in his face, his tiny little lips and his tiny hands, Neil had to swallow. When he looked up, Candy was watching him closely. "If you don't go now and lie down, Brad will be here, and then I'll have to leave. I don't want to leave you like this. I'll worry." He said it more sharply than he'd meant to, but he was unraveling inside, right here, right now, in front of his wife. He prayed not one shred of his anguish showed on his face.

"And Cat?" She touched the little girl's head, and Cat gazed up at Candy with love as she stood on her tiptoes, reaching for her.

"Cat, you stay here with Daddy," Neil said, and he reached for her hand before Candy could pick her up. "Go on, Candy."

He watched as she started up the stairs, stopping halfway up and gripping the railing as if she was expecting him to change his mind. "Go," he said again.

This time, she continued up to the second floor and into the master bedroom at the top of the stairs; he let out a breath in relief. Hiding his feelings, keeping the secret of Michael, the baby who was truly his, was causing everything to unravel around him. How long could he keep it buried? Forever, if it was up to him, but he was a realist, and he knew his brother and father were right when they said Candy would figure it out. She was a smart woman. Soon, she'd be asking him specific questions, ones he didn't want to answer. No, his family was right. He was running out of time—and it would be better if the truth came from him.

When he got back with her horse, donkey, and all their belongings, in the days before Christmas, he would tell her. Yes, that would work. It would give him time to get used to the idea and come up with the best strategy to come clean.

Chapter 3

"Let's go and see if Brad is here yet," Candy said. She had the baby fastened in a snuggly to her front, and she slipped her dark coat on but left it open. She touched the knitted hat on Michael's head, covering his downy dark hair, and tucked a blanket over him. Cat was in a red coat, her hood up, and she stuck her feet in identical red gumboots. "Are you coming?" Candy asked the girl as she opened the door and stepped onto the concrete step that Neil had exposed when he took apart the front deck after discovering rot and insisting on rebuilding it himself.

Candy held out her hand until Cat slipped her tiny one into it. As she stepped outside into the unusual warmth, she wondered whether she'd overdressed Cat and the baby. The lack of sun, the dreary gray, had fooled her into thinking it was colder out.

She could hear the gate at the end of the driveway open, and she walked down the sidewalk and spotted Brad and Emily's black truck pulling in and parking in front of the detached double garage, which was beside the now filled woodshed away from the house. "Look, Cat, it's Emily!"

"Hi, there," Emily called out as she climbed out of their truck.

"I didn't know you were coming over." Candy kept walking, holding Cat's hand. There was one thing she'd noticed with Cat: She wasn't one to let go of Candy's hand or take off to run and play. She was cautious with Candy. It was different when Neil was around, as he was always playing with her, taking her hand and running with her across the wet grass, pulling her from her comfort zone. He was so good with her, and Candy could see how much he loved her. She just wished he felt the same about Michael.

Emily always looked so radiant. She was dressed casually in blue jeans, sneakers, and a black coat with a faux fur hood. It was new, a different look than her usual comfortable and warm attire.

"Love your new coat," Candy said as Emily approached, smiling ear to ear. She was absolutely glowing as she touched Michael's back, rubbing it before hugging Candy, careful not to squish the baby.

"I splurged," she said. "I saw it and had to buy it. I felt kind of guilty, as it's not really practical for the ranch."

"Emily, you're a beautiful woman. You don't have to explain it to me. I know you just want to look good for Brad. I have to tell you, though, that man only has eyes for you."

"Well, I know that. I'm still glowing from our holiday in the Greek islands. It was so special, and for the first time I dressed like a woman. It felt so good to know that I looked good for Brad, seeing the appreciation in his eyes. I just never admitted before now how much I needed that." Emily touched Cat's head and then bent down. "Hi, Cat! You look beautiful in that red coat and those boots."

"Daddy gone. I miss Daddy," Cat said, her voice flat. She signed to Emily as she talked.

"I know, but your daddy will be back soon. He'll be cutting it close to Christmas, won't he?"

"Three days before Christmas," Candy said, wishing for a moment that he'd waited until the new year for this trip. But Neil wasn't one to put anything off, and he'd been in an unusual hurry, it seemed, to close up everything and finish the move.

"Brad and I will keep you busy. There's so much Christmas in this community. There's they nativity pageant, Christmas shows, Santa Claus ..." she said. Cat frowned, still not understanding what any of that meant. Emily offered Candy a sympathetic smile. "How are you holding up?"

"Oh, I miss him even though he's only been gone a few hours. I'm used to having Neil here every day, and he does so much with Cat. Every waking moment, he has her engaged as he talks to her, reads to her, plays with her. There's so much he does here at the house. It's just that I'm in a new place with the kids, and ..." She stopped just short of saying she'd been checking the locks twice, listening to every creak of the floorboards. She didn't want Emily worrying about her.

"Are you nervous, being out here alone with the kids? You know you can come stay with us at the ranch. It'll be far from quiet and peaceful, but you won't be lonely. The girls would love to have Cat to play with and the baby to hold."

"Thanks, Emily, but I think I need to stay home. I have to get used to it. I'm just being silly. Before Neil and I were together, I lived alone and did everything myself. It's just that I never realized how much I'd started to depend on Neil. Did that happen with Brad?"

Emily raised her eyebrows and glanced away a second with a soft smile on her lips. "Oh, yes, and there was a time when I worried about how important he'd become in my life. He makes it so easy to lean on him, to let him handle everything, to the point that I really do worry that if something happened to him, I'd have to learn how to stand on my own two feet again. But I don't want to go there, to that place. I understand completely." She rubbed Candy's shoulder. "So where were you two off to?"

"To get some fresh air and wait for you outside. We haven't left the house today, and Neil has Cat outside with him every day while I'm inside with Michael. Speaking of which, this is the first time in weeks that Michael's relaxed." She rubbed her sleeping baby's back. "He's been so fussy. I think his tummy's been upset. He's always been so good up until now. He's had me up a few times in the night, and with Neil gone …" She shook her head.

"He may be teething, you know. Some babies really suffer—moms, too. Maybe you should come and stay with us. I can help with Michael if you're with us, and you know Brad will, too, and Katy really does want to babysit," Emily said, this time sounding worried.

"That is tempting, but I have to be able to stay here alone. This is ridiculous! I'm a grown woman."

"Of course you are, but everyone needs help, and it's different when you have a baby. Candy, you should lean on family, and we're here, close by. You just have to call us, day or night, you know that, right?"

It warmed her heart to realize she had people—no, family—who cared enough that they'd step in, no questions asked, and help. It was unsettling, and it touched her after being alone for so long. "I know, and I really am happy that you and Brad are so close."

Emily nodded but didn't push. "Did you want to take

Michael to the doctor and make sure there's nothing unusual going on? I can tag along, you know. With the kids in school all day, I have more time."

She started walking down the driveway, Emily beside her. "I do, actually. This is new for me, and I don't know much about Michael or his parents. Is this normal, is it just teething, or could there be something wrong? I've been wondering a lot lately."

Emily had a strange look on her face. She glanced away and reached for Cat's hand, and the little girl grabbed it. She wasn't about to walk alone. Candy could tell that her daughter missed Neil's comforting and reassuring presence.

"See?" she said. "Even Cat isn't as secure with Neil gone. What does that say about me?"

"Oh, don't start that. My kids do the same thing if Brad's gone. It's not the same without our watchdogs. Even I don't sleep well if he's not home. I listen to every sound and sleep so lightly. It goes with the territory. Thank goodness Brad doesn't go away often. Think about it, though. Maybe come for dinner tonight. Brad will come and get you, and if you don't want to stay over, he'll bring you home."

"Hmm, maybe," Candy said, hearing another truck at the gate.

"Ah, looks like the mail's here. Cat and I can race over there and grab it for you?" Emily said, looking down at Cat and then up at Candy.

"Sure, I'm not doing much running these days," Candy said.

She watched as Emily held her little girl's hand and encouraged her to run alongside her with careful, awkward steps to the mail box. It was slow, and she noticed how unsteady Cat was, not letting go of Emily's hand. Neil was always ready to catch her, and Cat must have known that this time was different. Candy realized then that she felt the same way. Having someone who loved her so much, who was so confident he could do, and handle, anything in life; who was always there, ready to catch her and pick her up, meant more than words could describe. The ten days until her husband came home would be ten of the longest she'd ever known, but then they could truly begin their new life here.

Chapter 3

"I miss you. I'm so glad you landed safely," Candy said into the cordless phone. She glanced at the baby in his swing, kicking his legs. Cat was on the floor, coloring.

"I told you I'd call as soon as I landed in Phoenix. How are the kids? Is Cat okay?"

It didn't surprise her it was Cat he asked about—never Michael, not by name.

"She misses her daddy. I'm taking Michael to the doctor tomorrow. Emily phoned, got the appointment. He's going to need Cat's medical records from Dr. Alvariz, too, and we'll have to find a new speech pathologist here, Neil."

"I'll call Dr. Alvariz here and take care of the records for Cat. And stop worrying. I can hear it in your voice. After Christmas, we'll get Cat started with someone to work on her speech. It's not going to hurt her to have a break, Candy. We've got the holidays to enjoy, and I'll be home soon."

How did he always know she was stressed even before

she did? Maybe it was in her voice. "How long will you be in Phoenix?" she asked. For a minute, she wished she was with him, even though it would be so much work to travel with the kids. She heard Neil say something to someone, and then he came back to the phone.

"I hope to be here just one night. I have movers meeting me at the apartment within the hour, and I'll leave them to pack up and ship everything to us. If all goes well, and I expect it will, I should be on a morning flight to Cancun. I plan to spend only a couple days there, finalizing some business, and then start back with Sable and Ambrose."

"Neil, drive safe. That's a long drive back, and I'm worried about you on the roads at this time of year. You have to come through the mountains, and there'll be snow. Please don't rush. Just stay safe."

He chuckled softly. "I'll be fine, Candy. I love you. Listen, I spoke with Brad and asked him to swing around and check on you, make sure you and the kids are okay." She could hear someone in the background, talking. "Candy, I've got to go. The cab driver is just pulling up in front of our place. I promise to call you later. Give Cat a big hug from me and tell her that her daddy misses her."

"And Michael?" she said. She was so tired of Neil's lack of interest in their son, even though he tried to deny it.

"Of course, Candy. I miss all of you, but he's a baby. Cat isn't. Michael needs you more. You're his mother."

That was fine, but she knew there was more to it. Now he sounded rushed.

"Listen, honey, I really have to go. I promise I'll call later. Maybe stay at the ranch with Brad and Emily? They can help out until I get back." He was sounding like Emily, and Candy wondered whether Brad would push the issue when he showed up to pick them up for dinner.

"You know what? I'll think about it, but I'm sure we'll be fine. I love you, too."

"I'm here, Candy. Call me if you need me." Then he hung up.

She held the phone, glad Neil had called. She found herself counting down the days, the hours, in her head until he'd be home. "Cat, that was Daddy on the phone. He said he misses you."

Cat gazed up at Candy, her tiny white teeth showing when she smiled. "Daddy come home?" she asked, still holding her crayon.

"No, not yet, Cat. Soon, though. Your Uncle Brad is coming to pick us up and feed us dinner. You can play with Katy and Becky. Won't that be fun?"

"Yeah," she said, then jumped up, racing to the window to wait.

"Cat, come finish coloring your picture."

"All done. I wait," she said.

Candy put the phone down on the sofa table, taking in the newspaper and stack of mail. "Come on, Cat. Uncle Brad won't be here for another hour yet. You can't stand there that long. Come on over here and I'll brush your hair; maybe you can find a new outfit to wear, something pink or red or …"

"Green!" Cat shouted. She loved that color, second to red.

"Okay, something green. I'm sure you have lots."

Cat raced over and bumped the sofa table, knocking off the phone and the papers. "Sorry, Mommy," she said, squatting down to pick up the papers. "Here, Mommy!" She handed an envelope to Candy and then reached for another, trying to be helpful. Candy couldn't get over how far she'd come from the little girl she'd found in a Mexican orphanage, a girl who couldn't hear, couldn't talk, and didn't understand what was happening to her.

"Thank you, sweetie," she said as she took the newspaper, all scrunched up with inserts hanging out. She set it down and glanced at a handwritten envelope sticking out of the side of the paper. That was unusual, as everything else was printed. She picked it up and glanced over at Cat. "Go clean up your crayons," she reminded her.

She glanced back at the envelope with the neat script in blue ink, addressed to Neil. The return address was in Mexico. "Who's writing you, Neil?" She turned the envelope and tapped it over her fingers. She was going to put it down when she noticed the name on the return address: M. Perez. She had to think for a moment as her stomach tightened. That was Maria, of course. That was her last name.

Candy ached with anger. How dare this woman write her husband? She'd had enough, and she slid her finger under the seal to open it, pulling out two sheets of paper, all in handwriting. "What do you want now, Maria?"

"Mommy, all done," Cat said, setting her crayon box on the sofa table atop the papers.

Candy had to pull her gaze away from the script to Cat. "Okay, honey, just give Mommy a minute." She glanced over at Michael, sound asleep in the swing, his head tilted to the side, sucking on his pacifier, then back to the pages she was holding.

Dear Neil,

I cry for my baby every day. I miss him so. I miss you, and I don't know how to reach you, as you won't take my calls. You changed your number. When I called your cell phone, it was disconnected. Why won't you call me? Why have you turned your back on me?

Candy glanced up at Cat, who was waiting for her. She

saw the reflection of headlights in the window before she heard Brad's truck. "There's your Uncle Brad. He's early."

Cat raced to the window, and Candy had to fight the urge to read what this woman wanted. Maria was mourning the miscarriage and still pining for Neil. Why hadn't he told her? It was pathetic, Candy couldn't help thinking, even though she understood all too well the ache of losing a baby. She went to crumple the paper. She needed to open the door, get Cat and the baby ready, but instead she looked back down at the handwriting.

Please, Neil, I beg you: Let me see my baby. Tell me how he is! Is he okay? I know he has your smile, your eyes.

What the hell? For a moment, everything seemed surreal. All that registered was the buzzing in her ears. She couldn't tear her eyes away from the letter even though she could hear the truck door slamming shut and Cat racing to the door. She was frozen on the spot.

All the money you've given us can't replace my son. I made a mistake. I want to be part of his life. You can't keep hiding him. Why would you move so far away and take my son? He is my blood, he is part of me and part of you. I am his mother. Please don't be so cruel
...

"Candy, are you ready?" Brad was in the doorway. She had never heard him step inside.

She stared across the room at him. He'd picked up Cat and was holding her, but it seemed as if he were somewhere else—or maybe it was her. Her throat was tight, and, for a moment, she forgot how to breathe. She gasped for air, and Brad's eyes widened. He hurried across the room to her.

"Candy, are you all right? What's wrong, Candy?" He put Cat down, and then he had his arm around her and was leading her to the sofa to sit her down. She realized she was shaking. "What's going on, Candy?" he asked, and he reached for the letter she was holding, but her hand was gripping it so tightly she couldn't let it go. "Candy, honey, what is going on? Is it bad news?"

Brad had his hands on her arms. He was holding her together, and he had such concern in his eyes. They were a deeper brown than her husband's, but they were so similar. His expression was different than Neil's—older, wiser, maybe that was it. The shape of his face was more square, and he had lines around his eyes that were deeper than Neil's. He was his brother, his older brother, a man Candy was fond of. She just stared at him, and then she was shaking her head. She tried to find something to say, but in the end she just held out the letter. Brad took it from her and started reading. She didn't miss the furrow in his brow, the shock in his expression. He shut his eyes, lowering the paper, and glanced away for a second. When he looked back at her, the sympathy on his face, in his eyes, made her want to weep.

"You already knew!" she cried out, because it was something he hadn't been able to hide.

Chapter 4

S he was crying, weeping, her hands covering her face. She just stood there, trying to hide her tears from her kids.

What could Brad say to Candy to make this better? Damn Neil! Why the hell hadn't he told her? He should have told her. It had been his responsibility, and, right now, Brad wanted to kick his brother's ass for putting him in this position and for the heartache that was written all over Candy's face. He didn't want to know about this horrible thing Neil had done. The fact was that Maria had written to his brother, and Candy had opened the letter. This was the worst, and he'd tried to warn his brother it could happen. He just hadn't imagined it would be like this.

"Candy, I am so sorry." He took in Cat, who was standing beside the sofa, just watching them. He could see how upsetting this was to her. "Hey, Cat," he said. "Your mommy is just sad about something, but she's okay, all right?" He put the letter on the coffee table and bent down to pick her up, and then Michael stirred in his swing. He kicked his legs and started whimpering.

"Candy …" He glanced back and saw her watching the baby. Her arms were crossed, her face red and tear stained, but the look in her eyes was haunting. She didn't move. "Cat, I need to get your brother," he said.

Cat became very quiet and touched her lip with her finger as she stood beside Brad. He reached in the swing, unbuckled the baby, and lifted him out. He was in striped, stretchy pajamas, and his bottom was wet. He'd leaked right through. "Not comfortable being wet, is it, buddy?" he said as he held the baby against his coat and patted his bottom. "Candy, I know you're upset, but the kids …" He let his meaning sink in. She ran her hand roughly under her eyes, sniffing and taking a deep breath.

"How could you know already?" she asked, but it came out like an accusation. She didn't reach for Michael, who was fussing and getting ready to let out a wail. She just stood there, her arms at her sides.

"Unfortunately, I wish I didn't, but now is not the time. Michael needs changing. Kids first, Candy. Do you want me to change him?" He could see her hesitation. There was a second in which she pulled into herself, as if that was the only way she could keep herself together and get through this moment. Then she stuck her arms out to take the baby.

"I'll get him changed. I just …" She looked around and then down at Cat. "I need to get Cat changed, too. Maybe we should stay here and not go to your place. I'd rather not." She sounded flustered.

"Katy, Becky!" Cat called out, as if she understood what Candy was saying.

"Cat's looking forward to seeing her cousins and playing with them," Brad said. "Go get Michael changed. Cat, don't worry. You're coming over, and the girls are excited and waiting to spoil you."

Candy said nothing more as she walked out of the room and up the stairs.

He glanced down at Cat with a heavy heart. This was the last thing he wanted for Neil and his family, but secrets and lies had a way of coming out—often in unexpected ways.

Candy remained silent when she returned with a freshly changed Michael. She pulled some warm pants on Cat, and, with both kids bundled up, Brad put them in their car seats in the back of his truck. Candy had pulled on a black coat and followed him out with a diaper bag over her shoulder; she stood quietly while Brad finished fastening the kids in. He closed the back door, and she glanced down at her hands. He knew she wanted to say something, but she seemed to be having trouble speaking.

"Why, Brad? How? I don't understand how you would know. Was this planned, this deception? Does everyone know, and I'm the only fool who doesn't? I...I ... explain this to me. Please." She had found her voice, all right. He could hear how rattled she was.

"I don't think it's right for me to talk about this, Candy. You need to talk to Neil."

The look she gave him, in that moment, let him know she was about to take her kids out of his truck and walk in the other direction.

"Come on, Candy," he said. "Get in the truck. It's cold out here."

She shook her head. If she were his wife, he'd have opened the door and lifted her in, but she wasn't. She was Neil's wife, his brother's wife; the brother who'd made a mess he now found himself having to deal with.

"Candy, you're not a fool," he said. "This wasn't some conspiracy, if that's what you're thinking. Neil was so upset when you came for Trevor's birthday, and I know my brother well. I pushed him to open up because I knew something was bothering him. I just had no idea it was this." He gestured with his hands as Candy watched him.

"When did you find out?" she asked.

"Not long afterward," he said, and she took another breath and nodded, then reached for the passenger door. Brad reached around her, touching her hand, pulling the door open, and helping her in. He stood there for a moment while she buckled her belt. "Candy, whatever is going through your head, don't shut us out. We're family, and I know better than anyone that when you close the door on someone because you're hurt and angry, and you cut them out of your life, it's your pride and not your heart that you're following. Don't do anything without talking things through first. There's a lot you don't know. Neil may have had his reasons for doing this——"

"He lied to me about that woman! He lied about Michael. There's no explanation, period. End of story, Brad." She actually went to unfasten her belt.

"Okay, stop. Let's just call a timeout right now. Let's go have dinner. We'll talk later." He didn't wait for her to say anything more, because she was too angry to be reasoned with. He just hoped that once he got her to the ranch and she had dinner and a chance to sit for a moment, she'd be in a better frame of mind to listen.

Chapter 5

Her chest ached, her head, her stomach. Her eyes burned. She sat beside Brad in his truck. She didn't know her brother-in-law well, but she liked and respected him. She didn't know what to say to cut through the betrayal she felt. The heater was running, filling the cab with warm air, but that did little to thaw the chill that was now flowing through her veins. She felt like a fool, an idiot, as if she were the butt of a joke. She knew Brad kept glancing her way. She could hear the way he ran his hand over his chin as if thinking of a way to make her feel better.

"Don't, Brad. Just don't," she said, keeping her eyes on the dim road. The sun was setting, and there were thick clouds overhead. It had started raining again.

"Candy, this wasn't the way for you to find out. I'm pretty sure I don't know everything, but I do know Neil loves you and he would do anything for you. That's why he moved you up here and away—"

"He was hiding us," she said. "He created a situation and thought he could move us so far away it wouldn't touch us." She didn't want to hear Brad's excuses, and she listened to him sigh as he turned down the driveway of his acreage and up to the white two-story family home. At one time, it had seemed so welcoming, as if Candy could go there anytime and be part of something bigger. For the first time, she'd begun to believe she was part of a family.

"Who else knows?" she asked as Brad parked between a minivan and a tractor. He turned off the truck and slid around to glance back at the kids, and she could tell by the strain in his face and the tic in his cheek that there was more she wasn't going to like. "Emily?" she said. Please, no, not Emily, her friend and the one person in the family who had always been there for her.

"Let's get the kids inside, Candy. This isn't something Cat should hear."

She shut her eyes and wanted to weep again; the ache was almost unbearable. Of course Emily knew. Brad wasn't a liar. He probably told his wife everything. How different could two brothers be?

He shut the door and walked around the back to lift Cat out of her car seat. He was talking to the kids, but she couldn't really make out what he was saying. When she stepped out just as Brad closed the back door, Michael was nestled in the crook of his arm and Cat was standing beside him, her tiny hand clutching his jeans. Her little girl had picked up on everything, of course. Candy reached down to take her hand when she heard the screen door squeak open.

"There you are! I was wondering if something had happened. I was about to call your cell phone to see if everything was okay." Emily was rubbing her arms as she stepped out on the porch in a long-sleeved peach shirt, dark blue jeans, and black slippers on her feet. But the expression on her face changed from happy to guarded as she looked first to Brad and then to Candy.

"Candy, come on. Let's go inside," Brad said as he started toward the house, carrying Michael. Candy took her time and reached in the truck for the diaper bag, having to turn away from Emily and Brad. She took Cat's hand again and started for the door. She didn't look up, but the energy around them was tense. She heard a whisper as Brad stepped beside Emily, and she glanced up, taking in the moment between them and watching as Emily flushed with color. She shut her eyes and was about to say something before she realized Cat was still watching them.

"Cat, the girls are waiting for you," Emily said. She didn't say anything else, which Candy was glad for at that moment—though, she was also angry that Emily hadn't immediately apologized. Making it worse were the hundreds of suspicions flooding her mind. Was there some kind of conspiracy among the people who were supposed to care about her?

Candy stepped into the house and watched as her two nieces pulled Cat away. They were chattering and climbing the stairs, excited to have the little girl over. Brad was standing just inside the room, holding Michael the way Neil should have but never did.

"Candy ..." Emily began. Her friend and sister-in-law held her hands together and then gestured helplessly. "I can only imagine how you feel. How did you find out?" she said, though she looked to Brad.

"Candy got a letter in the mail from the surrogate." Brad left out how Maria had pleaded to see Neil, to see Michael.

"She wants him back," Candy said. "Neil lied to me, told me Maria lost the baby. Then there was a baby for us, and he let me believe Michael had just appeared, ready for adoption. What I don't understand, Emily, is how you kept this from me. What, did you all have a big laugh behind my back about what a fool I am?" Her throat tightened, and tears burned her eyes again. At some point in the past hour, her heart had shattered into a million pieces over this betrayal. How could a man she loved so deeply deceive her this way?

"Candy, Emily wanted to tell you, but I said no even though you had every right to know," Brad said. "It had to come from Neil. He said he was going to tell you, and even Dad told him——"

"Rodney knows?" she shouted. "Oh my good God, did everyone in this family know what Neil had done except me?"

Emily glanced to Brad and then stepped around Candy to close the door. She put her hand on Candy's shoulder, but Candy couldn't stand the touch and moved away.

"Please don't," she said. That hurt Emily's feelings, of course, but right now she was in survival mode, and she would lash out and hurt anyone just to get through this.

"Mom figured it out and told Dad. It was the timing, Candy, and Michael resembles how Neil looked as a baby. Of course Mom would know, but no one else does, if that's what you're worried about." Brad looked so large, just like Neil, when he held a baby. Michael started to fuss again, and he rocked him and then glanced back over at Candy. "Candy, you need to talk with my brother. It shouldn't have come out this way. It's not fair to you, but, in Neil's defense, he seemed to think he was going to lose you. Instead of coming clean, he just kept digging a hole for himself. He loves you."

Emily was looking down at her hands. Her face was

tight, and she glanced back at Candy with sadness. "What are you going to do?"

She was standing in the doorway with her coat on, her hands in her pockets, staring at a baby she had believed was hers. She now realized that little boy could end up being lost to her. "I don't know what to do. I told Neil from the beginning that Maria was going to be a problem. Now this baby isn't even mine, and he could be taken away. For that, I will never forgive Neil."

Chapter 6

"I should probably go take Michael from Brad," Candy said. She was sitting on the sofa, her legs pulled up, her chin resting on her knees and her arms wrapped around her legs. She could hear the girls giggling and Brad in the kitchen with Katy and Trevor, cleaning up after dinner.

"Brad's fine," Emily said. "If he wanted you to take Michael, he'd be in here giving him to you." She sat beside Candy on the sofa, her arm over the back. But there was a space between them.

Brad walked in, holding Michael in the crook of his arm. Candy didn't miss how comfortable the baby was with him. His eyes were wide open, his tiny fists waving. "Emily, are you two okay?" He hovered for a moment and took in Candy. She wondered if he was worried she hated him.

Emily ran her hand over the back of her head and nodded. "We're good. Do you need help?"

The moment between them was so personal, a connection Candy longed to have with Neil. It was something that spoke of years together and knowing what the other was thinking. She felt as if she'd lost all the ground she'd covered with Neil, with this family. She was an outsider.

"I'll put on water?" Brad said. He waited a second, and Emily nodded.

"Thanks, Brad." She turned back to Candy, and Brad wandered back into the kitchen.

"Brad's good with babies," Emily said. "Besides, he wants to give you a minute. You were very upset before dinner, and you didn't eat much, if anything. I do know what it looks like when you move food around on your plate but don't take one bite."

"Lost my appetite," Candy said. "It's hard to eat when your heart is jammed in your throat. I have a hundred questions, and I don't know what to ask. Why?" She gestured aimlessly before gripping her legs again, squeezing until her arms started to ache. She knew Emily wanted to touch her hand. She saw how she hesitated before squeezing her fist and keeping her hand in her lap. "You know, when I woke up in the hospital and found out I had lost the baby, you were the one who stayed with me," Candy said. "Neil wasn't there. I understand now how hurt he was, and we moved past it, but that hurt, that abandon-ment … it stays with you. It leaves a scar on your soul. Why didn't you tell me that Neil told you about Michael? I mean, it had to have been difficult, being with me and the baby and not saying a word."

"Neil didn't tell me. He was furious that I'd found out," Emily said, sounding resigned.

"Oh?" How would she have known if Neil hadn't told her?

Emily glanced over her shoulder toward the kitchen and then back to Candy. "My husband tried to keep it from me. He was very upset. I'd never seen him like that.

He snapped at the kids and was short with me, so I knew something was wrong. You see, Brad was worried about Neil, said he'd been acting strangely. He planned to pull him aside when you got here and have a word with him so he could get to the bottom of what was going on. I don't think Neil intended to tell Brad, but they're close, Candy, even with this between them. And this …"

Emily waved her hand. "I'm telling you this has been a rift between Brad and Neil, and, from what I understand, Rodney, too." She shrugged. "I couldn't tell you, Candy. I wanted to. God knows I did. It had to come from Neil. We told him to talk to you. Brad was on his case to tell you, and, from what Brad said, he thought Neil *was* planning on telling you. Why did he stall?" She gestured again help-lessly. "I can only say he was afraid to tell you. I would be, too, if I'd done something like this. Please don't be angry with me. I can only imagine how betrayed you feel. I don't know how I'd feel if it were me." Emily appeared so sad.

Candy let go of her legs and slid around, facing Emily and touching her arm on the seatback. "I don't know what to do or what this means for me. Am I Michael's mother or not? Will I lose him now? What do I do?"

The floor creaked, and she glanced up at Brad, who was still holding Michael, now fast asleep. "I need to go out to lock everything up and check that the cattle and horses were fed."

Candy took in the worry in Brad's expression. Even though she was numb, she knew he and Emily cared.

"He's your child, Candy," Brad said then. "No one can tell you otherwise, certainly not a letter from a woman who set out to cause trouble. Of everything in this mess, you can count on that one thing. Michael is yours and Neil's." Brad slid Michael into her arms, and she found herself, for the first time, seeing Michael differently, looking for Maria, seeing Neil in him. How could she have missed it? She felt like such a fool.

Brad was still watching her when she looked up, and Emily reached over and touched the baby's foot lightly. "I understand better than anyone, Candy, raising a child you love as yours and knowing his birth mother is out there," she said.

Brad was still standing over her. "Candy, you need to talk to Neil, and you need to listen to him. What he did wasn't right, and I'm not excusing any of it. It was stupid and thoughtless and not one of his finest moments, but there was a lot more behind his motives that came from a fear of losing you. You should stay here tonight." He glanced to Emily.

"You shouldn't be alone tonight, Candy. Brad's right, you should stay here with us," she said, as if she and her husband were of the same mind.

"Look, I know you're both concerned, but I'm a big girl. I think it's best if I go home," Candy said, and she didn't miss the hardness in Brad's expression, as if he had realized he could only push so far with her. "If you wouldn't mind taking us home when you're done outside, I need to get Cat and Michael to bed," she added. She also needed time alone to absorb what had happened, to reread that letter, and to cry alone where no one would hear her.

"All right, let me finish up and I'll take you home," Brad said.

Emily reached for his hand as he started to walk away, and they exchanged a moment as he held her hand, her fingers, then let go. Theirs was an intimate closeness, a bond she longed for with Neil, but the sad truth was that whatever had been there between them had been nothing more than an illusion.

Chapter 7

Where was his phone? He could hear the ringing as he taped up a box of papers, invoices, expenses from the Cancun resort, everything he needed to send to the accountant. He always had his phone on him, but he must have set it down after the movers finished, after he had started searching for the black file he didn't want misplaced. He lifted his computer bag and the piles of mail that had been shoved under the door when he arrived. There was his cell phone, and his brother's name was on the screen. "Hey, Brad, what's up?" Where had he put that file with all the legal papers and the bank notes on Michael? It had a small lock so no one could happen onto it or read it—namely his wife.

"You have a problem," Brad said rather sharply.

He spotted another box, unmarked, and he started to open it as he only half listened to his brother. "And that would be"? He tucked the cell phone between his shoulder and ear and started opening the box.

"Candy knows about Michael."

It took him a second to understand what Brad was saying. "Candy knows what?" As soon as he said it, his stomach tightened and a strange coldness settled around him.

"There was a letter in the mail from that surrogate," Brad said. "Neil, I walked in to pick her and the kids up, and she was so upset."

He touched his head and gripped the phone as if his life depended on it. "You're telling me Maria sent a letter to my house? How the hell did she get my address"? His mind was racing. "What did the letter say? Did you read it"? God, how bad was it? *Oh, Candy, oh no—please don't hate me.*

"That woman is pining for you, Neil. I can't remember everything, but she wants to see her baby. She wants to talk to you. I guess I know why you have a new cell phone number now. Reading between the lines, Neil, I'd say you have some trouble. Maria wants her baby back, so tell me again how this surrogacy was such a good idea?" Brad could be a real prick when he wanted to.

"Was that all she said?" he asked. Why was Maria hell bent on trying to talk to him, trying to rip apart his life with Candy? When she tried to reach him through his lawyer, Les, he'd paid her five million to go away. The signed contract was in the black file he needed to find. He had given her everything he had left, which was the reason he now needed to sell the resort. He no longer had the cash to run the operation, and Maria was a huge problem that just wouldn't go away. Why hadn't he listened to Candy? She had been so right about Maria and her mother, Carmen, but that hadn't been the first time he was blinded by the need to have a child of his own. It had been careless, and he'd opened himself up to this nightmare that just wouldn't end.

"Where is Candy now"? He was drowning from the panic licking the back of his throat. She was so far away, and it would take too long to get back home, to get to her ...

"She's at home. Em and I tried to get her to stay here with us, but she wouldn't. She was really angry at Emily, too, and at me, for knowing about it. She feels betrayed. My wife is upset now, worried about Candy and what she's going to do."

It was quiet on Brad's end. Neil found himself listening, trying to pick up the sounds of home, something that would help him and keep him from wanting to pull all his hair out. "What do you mean, what she's going to do? Did she say something?" Was she going to leave? Would this be the end? He couldn't bear the thought, and he wanted Brad to tell him everything. He needed to race back to the airport and get on the next flight home. He was pacing the floor, feeling the short Berber carpet on his bare feet.

"No, she's completely thrown, Neil. She kept saying she didn't know what to do. You need to turn around and come home. I don't know how you're going to fix this. I've never seen the look she had on her face before. Even when she had the hysterectomy, that was a rough time, but, now, Neil ... she looked lost." Brad sounded tired all of a sudden.

"I'm on my way. I'll get on the first flight back. Could you stay with Candy, have Emily go over or something, please?" He would beg if he had to. Someone had to stay with her until he got back.

"I planned on going over in the morning. There's no way she'll allow anyone to stay with her tonight. We'll go first thing. Emily wants to go over to stay with her after taking the kids to school. They were supposed to go the doctor's tomorrow, an appointment for Michael or something. Neil, I don't want to say I told you so, but this time you fucked up big. I don't know how you're going to dig your way out of this one. She loves you, but, sometimes, when someone deceives you, love can turn to hate. I know. I've been there."

He let his brother's meaning sink in. He understood his brother's hate for his ex-wife, Crystal, who had lied and cheated and been a miserable excuse for a wife, abandoning her son as a baby. But did that compare to him? He couldn't think of that right now. "Thanks, Brad," he said. "I'll call you and let you know when I'm coming."

He didn't know how long he stood there, looking around the empty apartment and then at the box he'd just opened. He saw the black plastic and pulled at the corner of the file tucked down the side of the box. It held everything he needed, what he'd been looking for to protect his family, but it did little to comfort him now. All he could hear was the pounding of his heart and his strained breathing.

Chapter 8

It was dark, and the only reason she knew it was morning was that the digital clock beside the bed was flashing 5:23 a.m. She had cried off and on most of the night, clutching a pillow in her arms and holding it so tight she felt stiff in every bone. She ached with grief, with heartache, and it took every ounce of will to take her next breath. She waited in the dark, lying there as the seconds ticked by. The phone had rung for hours and hours the night before, over and over. Each time, the caller ID had shown it was Neil.

Of course Brad had called him. It was only a matter of time. She had expected this, expected the calls, but she couldn't speak with a man who'd turned her life upside down and left her feeling empty. She didn't want to hear his excuses, his lies, his sweet talking. She just couldn't listen to one word from him right now. So she let it ring. It had stopped at midnight, and for five hours she'd waited for it to ring again. But it hadn't.

She needed to think, and lying here in a bed she shared with Neil, a bed where his scent lingered, only added to her confusion. Neil was everywhere in this room. She climbed out of bed and pulled on her housecoat, a dark blue, fluffy one with a hood. It was hanging on a hook next to Neil's, and she went to touch his. She often slipped it on just to feel him around her, except now she couldn't bear to have it touching her skin.

She wandered down the carpeted hall, the faint night-light cutting through the darkness. She looked down into the living room, seeing the outline of furniture, and stopped outside Cat's open door. She was asleep in her twin bed, the stuffed animals and dolls Neil had bought her tucked in the beanbag chair beside the bed. Everything in here, Neil had bought it for her. Candy wondered, as she stared at her daughter. Neil had wanted nothing to do with Cat when Candy found her in that orphanage, and now he was a loving, doting father. What had happened, what had changed? He had originally moved her and Cat to Arizona, abandoning his own child—or had he? She had so many questions. She needed answers from the one man she had no desire to talk to right now.

She rested her hand on the doorframe and tried to absorb this lovely house Neil had bought, this house he owned. She didn't know what she was going to do. Everything was in Neil's name, his money, his credit cards. She had nothing. She never had, and it was disconcerting to realize how much she depended on him. She wondered when Michael, the baby she thought of as hers, would be ripped from her arms. It always came back to Maria, a woman Neil had brought into their lives, like a poison that slowly destroyed everything Candy believed was real.

She wandered into the baby's room and watched him sleeping soundly in his crib. He'd kicked the blankets off again and was now lying just in his terry sleeper, sucking on his pacifier, making soft little squeaks. She carefully pulled the blanket from under his foot and covered him. She ran her hand softly over his tummy, and her heart nearly broke in two at the thought of another woman coming in and taking her child. No, there was no way. Michael was hers. She loved him. He'd been hers since he was a few days old. She knew every detail of him, the shape of his toes, how he gripped her fingers when she touched him, how he giggled when she tickled him, the soft stretching sounds he made when he first woke, and how he fought sleep when he was overtired.

"She can't have you back," she whispered, and she stood there watching her baby until the light of the rising sun cut through the darkness. She stepped out of his room and down the stairs. She was halfway down when she heard a key in the lock, and she froze, touching her chest as the fear hit. Was someone breaking into her house? Before she could get her legs to move and flee back up the stairs, the door opened, and she saw the outline of him, his dark hair, and his leather coat. He flicked on the light, and she stared into her husband's eyes as he watched her watching him.

Chapter 9

Neil had pulled every string he could. He'd traded favors and paid a fortune, racking up his credit card debt to get a seat on a flight back to Seattle. He'd ended up chartering a helicopter to get him the rest of the way home, and it had landed at Grays Harbor just after 5:00 a.m. Brad, whom he'd woken up, had been waiting there.

Neil hadn't slept. How could he, after the bomb his brother had dropped? He'd called Candy again and again, and not once had she answered the phone. Of course he was freaking out. Was she there, or had she packed up and left with his kids? Where would she go? He wondered if she was so angry she wasn't going to take his calls. She had to know it was him calling. No, face to face was better. Then he could make her listen, but how could he get her to understand that he'd done this out of a twisted sense of love for her?

Neil stood in the open doorway and then shut the door as he watched his wife lingering on the stairs. Her expression reflected an agony he'd have given anything to take away. She said nothing as she stared at him, and he could feel the wall she was erecting between them.

He put down his bag, tossed the keys on the table by the door. She still hadn't moved. Her long, dark hair was a tangled mess, and her eyes were swollen and puffy from the tears she must have cried.

"I'm so sorry" was all he could say as he started toward her.

Then she crumpled where she stood halfway down the stairs.

It was instinctive for him to rush to her, to hold her, but she must have known, as she put her hands up just as his foot touched the first stair. "No, don't touch me," she said. "You don't get to touch me or hold me or lie to me again. Why did you do it?" She sniffed and breathed in deeply through her nose.

He could see her shaking, and he stopped himself from taking another step on the stairs. "I didn't want you to find out this way. If I'd had my way, you would never have found out, but I knew that was unrealistic. I planned to tell you when I got back from Mexico. I just had to find a way to keep you from hating me."

She was watching him with her mouth open as if getting ready to say something, but she was shaking from rage, anger, despair, sorrow—or all of it. She kept looking and searching him as if trying to figure out who he was.

"I need you to listen to me." He shut his eyes. "I was desperate. I thought I'd lost you to Cat."

Her eyes instantly filled with such fury he thought she'd walk right out the door or ask him to leave. He could feel the door closing between them and knew she didn't want to listen to one more word he had to say.

"Candy, I know I screwed up with Maria," he continued, "but I was so desperate to have a child that I wasn't seeing all the problems like you were. I thought Maria would have the child and honor the agreement. I didn't see how her interest in me was anything other than friendly, and I couldn't lose you. I walked away from them for you, for Cat." He was making a mess of this. He was a smooth talker when he wanted to be, but, for the life of him, he couldn't spin anything reasonable out of this mess.

Candy glanced away and then shook her head as she started down the stairs. Her feet were bare. She stopped just out of reach until he moved back and gave her space to slip by. He wanted to reach out and touch her, to pull her into his arms and hold her and promise her everything would be okay, that he'd make it okay. But he feared that his touch would never be welcome again.

"You walked away from Michael for me, for Cat? As I remember, you never wanted Cat. You were so angry at me when I went to the orphanage and furious at me for everything I did to help her. You did everything you could to stop me from spending time with her, from helping her. Then all of a sudden you were flying us to Arizona, and I watched you with her over those weeks in the hospital after the surgery, how you came around and you finally opened your heart to her. At the same time, you told me your baby died. You said Maria lost the baby, but Michael didn't die. He was growing inside Maria still!"

Candy stopped at the thermostat on the wall and flicked it on. "When that call came—and I remember it well, Neil—you said there was a baby for us, but Maria was the one who had the baby, right? You still didn't come clean. You lied. Now Maria wants her baby back, my baby!" She reached for some papers lying crumpled on the sofa table and shoved them at him.

He took the two loose-leaf sheets, handwritten: a letter

from Maria. How had she found him? He realized then that with what he'd paid her, it wouldn't have been hard for her to hire the right person, and they wouldn't have had to do too much digging. After all, he'd just bought a house, and the papers for the sale were easily traceable.

"So, Neil, is this adoption even legal? It's not final yet, is all I know. Will it ever be? God, I am such an idiot. What did you think would happen to me when she showed up and wanted her baby back?" Candy shouted the last part, clutching her chest. Her eyes were filled with such despair and hurt, such true torment.

"She won't get him back, ever. I can promise you that," he said as calmly as he could, taking a careful step toward her.

She stepped to the side and back so she was out of reach. "You can't promise me! I'm not that much of a fool, Neil. You've lied to me over and over. I can't trust anything you say. What else have you lied about?" She jammed her hands in her tangled hair and shoved it back.

He just looked at her, trying to figure out how this situation had gotten this bad. He hadn't expected anything like this. "Candy, I haven't lied to you about anything else, I promise—"

"Stop it with your damn promises! I don't want to hear it anymore. All your promises are lies." She actually picked up a crystal horse figurine and launched it at him. He ducked, and it shattered against the wall. Then there was a cry from upstairs—the baby.

Candy just stood there, shaking, breathing in and out so hard that she was out of breath. A tear slid down her cheek, and then she turned to go up the stairs and stopped on the second step. "I want you to leave," she said without looking back before continuing up into the baby's room.

Neil just stood there, holding Maria's letter, feeling his world, everything he'd created, everything he loved and controlled, crashing down around him.

Chapter 10

He was still here. She'd asked him to leave, and she was dying for saying it, but he'd made no move to leave this house, his house. She walked downstairs, carrying the baby after she'd changed him, and Neil had already heated a bottle for him. It was sitting in the bottle warmer, and a pot of coffee was brewing.

He held out his arms and said, "Why don't I feed him?"

Seriously? At any other time before today, she would have been jumping for joy. He'd never fed Michael his bottle, not once.

She turned and reached for the bottle to test the warmth. "No."

Michael reached for his breakfast. He sucked and swallowed while she walked away from Neil into the living room and sat in the glider rocker. She didn't need to look up to know Neil had followed her. There was something about his energy that always took over a room.

He sat on the edge of the table in front of her. She tried not to look at him, but he was like a drug. He leaned forward, his arms on his knees, his hands clasped between his legs.

"You're still here," she said. "Why haven't you left? Why won't you leave me be?"

He shut his eyes for a second as if her words were cutting into his heart. Of course they had been cruel, but she was desperate. She was doing everything she could to keep her head above water and not drown.

"I love you. I'm not going to walk out that door. I made a vow to you. We have a family, and I'll do whatever it takes to make this right with you."

At times, he could be immovable, and she sensed that now. However, she also saw a vulnerability in him that she'd never known existed. "I don't trust you," she said. "You lied to me. What else have you lied about, Neil? Tell me, please."

He shook his head and looked deeply wounded. "I kept a horrible secret, and I'm so sorry, but I never deliberately tried to deceive you."

She nodded, but she didn't understand. "Tell me, what else have you kept from me in this disgusting situation you created with Maria?"

He looked so calm and took a deep breath. "I paid Maria five million to go away. I had her sign away her parental rights. I have the agreement. Other than the resort and a few stocks I haven't sold, we're broke."

Was he serious? "Broke" was not something that went along with "Neil Friessen." Not that she cared about money, but she was stunned that he'd just tossed that amount to a woman, all for Michael. "So you bought Michael?" she said.

He glanced away. She wondered if he was trying to come up with some spin on the story to make it sound better. "I didn't buy Michael," he began. "That wasn't my intent. I wanted Maria and her mother to go away. I paid them to leave us alone."

She knew there had to be more, but she said nothing. She was done pulling teeth, trying to get him to tell her everything.

"I bought them a house. I paid for Maria's expenses. I paid Maria and her mother money, and they still wanted more. She wanted me. You were right, and I never saw it." He rubbed his hand over his chin. He was starting to get annoyed, and he sounded frustrated.

She rocked Michael slowly back and forth as he drank his bottle. This time, she didn't miss the way Neil watched him. "So why did you treat Michael as if he meant nothing to you? You gave all your attention to Cat, everything to a little girl you didn't want. Yet Michael is yours, and you gave him nothing. I'm not a fool, Neil. I noticed, I wondered, and I thought it was because he wasn't yours— but then, neither is Cat." She shrugged and shook her head. "Why?"

His expression was no longer guarded, and she wondered at the lightness in his amber eyes. Were those tears she was now seeing? Then he blinked. "I, uh ..." He cleared his throat. "It just about killed me with Michael. I knew I couldn't hide who he was, and I wasn't ready for you to know. I was just trying to get through each day, praying it would get easier. And Cat, she's my little girl, and I hope every day she never finds out what a bastard I was. I had such tunnel vision over wanting a baby that I was willing to look the other way while she rotted in an orphanage. At the time, I resented her for taking you away from me."

She couldn't believe he'd said that, that he'd thought that.

"I love her so much," he said. "The first time I realized

what she meant was when that nurse came in to give her a shot before surgery, and she was so scared she grabbed me with both her tiny fists. She didn't understand what was going to happen. I almost put an end to it there. It was like magic with Cat, and as the days passed, Maria and the baby were a thought in the back of my mind that I began to resent. But you and Cat were very much—*are* very much my life, my future."

What kind of future was there when the man she loved was built on a fantasy, and the solid foundation of their marriage was disintegrating from the lies? It was nothing. The entire fairytale was crumbling around them now. "What kind of future do we have?" she said.

"Don't say that. Candy, I would do anything for you, for our family. Don't walk away. Please give me a chance to make it up to you. I love you, and I don't want to lose you. I won't lose you!" He reached over to touch her, and she felt herself pulling away. Maybe he knew she couldn't stand to be touched, as he gently lowered his hand to her knee and then pulled it away. He must have felt her stiffen.

"One thing has nearly destroyed us over and over, and that was—*is* your need for children," she said. "You wanted them so badly that I really believed I was replaceable, and if you were honest with yourself, Neil, you'd realize you were willing to toss me away."

"Oh my God, you really believe that? You're not replaceable. You are the only woman I've ever loved. I have never wanted anyone else! You're my wife, you're mine …"

"Daddy!" Cat called out from the stairs and raced down to him. Candy didn't miss the way her face lit up, and Neil's, too. She leaped to him, and he grabbed her, pulling her into his lap and holding her, kissing her face. She giggled and then signed to him. She was so excited she had forgotten to talk. Neil rested his head atop Cat's and looked over at Candy, and what she saw in his eyes was the love of a father for his daughter. But what was worse was the truth he couldn't hide: his love for Michael, and the fact that he'd spent months deceiving her.

"You hungry?" he signed back to Cat, touching the back of her ear, as she didn't have the implant fastened. She signed back to him and then glanced over at Candy. "I'll get Cat breakfast," he said. "I'll make you something, too." He stood up with Cat in his arms.

"So you won't leave"?

He shook his head. "I'm not leaving. This is my family. You're my wife. We can't fix anything if I'm not here." He tightened his hold around Cat, who was watching Candy with apprehension. She wasn't the bad guy here. Cat was holding on to Neil as if everything in her tiny little life centered around him. She depended on him. As Candy watched her daughter and saw how much she loved Neil, she realized Cat believed he would protect her from everything.

If only that were true.

Chapter 11

"Emily is coming with me to the doctor," Candy said. She was dressed in dark pants and a matching sweater, her hair pulled back in a ponytail. Neil was holding Michael, and Cat was at the table, eating a second bowl of cereal.

"She doesn't need to. I'm here now," he said, and she flashed him with the "Drop dead" look she'd often given him before they dated, when she believed all the lies her father had told her about him.

"No, I don't want you there," she said, and she waited until he moved aside before reaching for a mug to pour herself a coffee.

"You need to eat something, Candy. I can make you some breakfast," he said, but she just shook her head.

"No, thank you. If I'm hungry, I can make it myself." She wasn't going to give an inch.

There was a knock at the front door, and then it opened. "Hello?" Emily called out as she stepped inside, the floor squeaking. The door clicked closed.

"In the kitchen, Emily," Neil said. When he stepped around the corner, he saw the surprise on Emily's face.

"How is … ?" She gestured to the kitchen, and Neil just shut his eyes and shook his head. Emily stopped in front of him and touched his arm. "Oh, Neil, I'm sorry. I don't know how you'll make this right."

"Seriously, Emily, make this right?" Candy stepped into the living room. The anger rolled off her as she took a swallow of coffee and set down her cup. She had puffy eyes, bloodshot. Neil knew she was tired and beyond being reasoned with.

Candy pulled open the closet door, and Emily glanced over at her and back to Neil. She then reached out her arms. "Why don't I hold the baby?"

Neil slid Michael in her arms as Candy pulled on her down coat, the white one, and shoved her feet into a pair of flats. He stepped in the doorway to the kitchen. "Cat, come on. We're going to take Michael to see the doctor." When he stepped back in the living room, Candy was wrapping a scarf around her neck, and Emily was saying something to her he couldn't make out.

"Maybe it would be best if I went alone with Candy," Emily said, worrying her lip between her teeth.

"Nonsense, we'll all go," he said, though he realized he wasn't winning any points by pushing.

***

CANDY COULDN'T DO THIS. Neil was being a stubborn ass. Didn't he get the fact that she didn't want to be around him?

She was sitting in the doctor's office, Neil holding Michael in his arms in the seat beside her, and Emily was on the floor in the corner with Cat, pretending to play with the toys. She wondered if everyone in this waiting room could pick up on the arctic temperature between her and Neil.

"Michael Friessen?" a nurse called out, holding a file.

Neil stood up with Michael, and Emily said, "Why don't I stay here with Cat?" She widened her eyes to Candy, who realized it probably seemed like she was going to have a hissy fit as she stood up behind Neil. He stopped at the doorway like a gentleman so she could go first, and she could feel him watching her. She didn't want to look at him, so she stepped around him and into the exam room. The nurse shoved the file in the compartment outside the door and then shut it, leaving Candy alone with her husband.

"Why don't you take the chair?" he said, gesturing to the only chair beside the exam table, but she didn't want to make things easier for him. In fact, she didn't want him here now, so she ignored him and went across the tiny exam room to stand beside the counter where all the doctor's supplies were.

Neil let out a weary breath as if she was pushing all his buttons, and she wondered if he was about to say something to her. Then the door opened and a tall man in brown dress pants, a striped dress shirt, and a tie strode in. He had dark-rimmed glasses, and he was looking at the file. He smiled when he took in Candy and Neil and shut the door behind him. "So is this Michael? What seems to be the problem?" He reached for the baby and laid him on the exam table, reaching for the stethoscope around his neck and rubbing the metal so it wouldn't be so icy cold on Michael's skin.

"He's been really fussy for weeks. Hasn't been sleeping well, has been throwing up," Candy said, her arms crossed.

Her back ached from the strain of being in the same room with Neil.

"How's Mom sleeping?" the doctor asked.

Candy was startled. What did that have to do with anything? "Fine, when Michael lets me." She didn't mean to sound so cross, but, then, she wasn't about to share with the doctor how she hadn't slept at all last night.

"How old is Michael"?

"Just over four months. He's seventeen weeks." She glanced at Neil.

The doctor unfastened his sleeper and listened to his heart. "That sounds really good and strong. Was it an easy delivery?" he asked, looking at Candy and then Neil.

"He's adopted, from a surrogate. I'm the biological father," Neil said.

"I can't have children," Candy added, and she noticed the look of concern on the doctor's face.

"Well, let me weigh him." The doctor ran his finger inside Michael's mouth, over his gums. "Ah, there we go. He's teething. With some babies, it can make them uncomfortable, but let's make sure there's nothing else going on. We'll run a few tests, but this little guy looks good."

Great, now how soon could she get out of this tiny exam room and away from her husband?

Chapter 12

She'd been circling him for days, five days of living under the same roof with a man she loved so deeply, a man she couldn't trust. He'd refused to leave, and she was angry at him for making her feel like the bad guy. She knew Cat wouldn't be okay if he left, but how could she live with a man, stay married to a man, who had deceived her as Neil had?

She could hear giggling from the living room, where Neil had dragged in a Christmas tree. He'd taken Cat with him to buy it, and he was explaining to her the scientific art of hanging ornaments on the branches. She stood in the archway and took in Michael in his swing, going back and forth beside Neil, kicking his legs and then giggling a big belly laugh when Neil stopped every few moments to tickle him. It was as if he was making up for the lost time of ignoring Michael for months.

She heard a vehicle pull in but didn't move as the doors shut. She knew it was Brad, Emily, and the kids. Neil had asked them to come. She said nothing.

The door opened after a knock, and Neil shouted, "Come in!"

"Hey, everyone. Wow, look at that tree," Emily said as she glanced at Neil, Cat, and Michael and then over to Candy, who was leaning in the kitchen doorway. She held a mug of coffee and took another sip as she tried to find something, anything, that could motivate her to be civil. The kids didn't seem to notice. Katy and Becky dropped their coats, kicked off their boots, and left them in a heap at the door. Trevor looked as if he'd grown again. His hair was combed so neatly, and he slipped off his coat, opened the closet, and pulled out a hanger. His boots he moved neatly to the side.

"Trevor, go help decorate the tree," Emily said. Brad was standing by the door, watching over his family, before his gaze lingered on Neil and then over to Candy as if he was trying to figure out what was going on. He patted his son's shoulder, and Trevor looked up and then walked over to the tree. Brad slipped off his own coat and hung it on a hanger. "That's a huge tree," he said, gesturing for Emily's coat, which he hung up as she walked over to Candy.

"Hmm," she replied. Of course it was still tense between them. She couldn't shake the fact that she felt her friend had picked Neil over her. She wasn't being fair, but she now believed she would always come second. "Coffee, hot chocolate?" she asked Emily. She would probably make some for the kids—hot chocolate, anyway—but she couldn't find anything joyous in this occasion.

Emily glanced over her shoulder at Brad, who shoved his hands in his jeans pocket and then tilted his head toward Neil and the kids. Whatever that meant, it seemed private between Emily and Brad. "Why don't I help you?" Emily said, touching Candy's shoulder and then following her into the open kitchen, setting a pair of gloves on the center island. The kitchen was nicely done in warm peach tones, and the large oval table was surrounded by six hard-back chairs. It was neat and tidy, just the way Neil liked everything.

Candy opened the fridge and just stared at the stocked shelf before lifting out a carton of milk. Emily was watching her, worrying her lower lip again between her teeth.

"Are you okay?" Emily asked.

Candy glanced over her shoulder to where she could see Neil pulling out ornaments and handing one to Cat. "Not really, but what can I say?" she said quietly enough that no one in the living room would hear.

Emily glanced over at Neil and then stepped around the center island, closer to Candy. Emily fisted her hand and then hesitated before opening it to touch Candy's. "I'm sorry. None of this is okay. Have you and Neil talked?"

Talked? That was all they'd been doing: fighting, not resolving anything. Neil assured her Michael would be theirs, that Maria couldn't possibly come in and take him because of the agreement she'd signed. He'd even shown her a black file with the agreement, but that didn't change the fact that the woman was a skeleton that would always lurk in their closets.

"Neil wants me to forgive him, to just go on as we were, but that's impossible," she said. The truth was that she'd made plans and seen a lawyer two days ago in town. He said he knew the Friessens, was a friend of Brad's, and he'd listened to her, anyway. What did she have to lose?

"Sometimes men find it easier to just ignore things instead of addressing the issue," Emily said. "Brad and I didn't have it easy in the beginning. I felt as if he turned his back on me when his wife showed up, and he had, thinking for some ridiculous reason that he was doing the right thing. But sometimes that right thing is so wrong, especially when it hurts the ones you love." Emily gripped Candy's shoulder. "You know that whatever you tell me, I won't betray your confidence."

Candy had to look away. She couldn't tell Emily she was looking at her options for the kids, where she stood legally as Michael's mother, and how she could look after the children if she left. The problem was—just as her potential lawyer, Keith, had said—that there were a lot of gray areas, especially since it seemed the adoption was not quite final. With Neil being the birth father, there was a lot of uncertainty, and it could be tough. Of course he wanted to see the papers, none of which Candy had, because they were in that black file that Neil kept locked.

"I just need to get through Christmas," Candy said. "But how do you live with a man you can't trust?"

Emily appeared embarrassed and shook her head. She stepped closer. "Look, in all fairness, I'm on the outside, seeing the situation without the same feelings of betrayal you're feeling right now. I don't know, if it was me, what I'd do. I know Neil loves you and the kids. He's family, and so are you, and of course I want it to work out between you, for everything to be okay for you, and for Cat and Michael."

The house phone was ringing, but Candy ignored it. There really wasn't anyone she wanted to talk to. She could hear Neil's voice, his laughter with Cat, and the kids' voices, how excited they were.

"I wish it were all that simple, Emily, to just forgive and move on, but I can't, not for something like this. There's just so many lies, all because of a baby, that innocent little baby in there, and his entire life is centered around a deception. I don't know what to do, but I'm also stuck on what I can't do. I can't walk away from Michael." She shook her head as she took in the shock in Emily's eyes. "No, I'm not leaving. I couldn't leave Cat and Michael. It would be easier to cut out my heart, I think. But Neil, he's already made it clear he won't leave, so I may have to—"

"Candy." Neil was standing in the kitchen. Brad was behind him, immediately going to Emily.

"That was Dad," Brad said. "Mom just had a stroke."

Candy heard Emily gasp and cry out, and she was in Brad's arms, and he was holding her, comforting her. Neil just stood across the room with an agony in his expression that she wouldn't wish on her worst enemy. She wanted to go over and hug him, touch him, but she didn't think her heart could take it.

Chapter 13

For ten long seconds, she'd considered staying home. She'd considered telling Neil to leave her and the children and get on a plane to Cancun without her. But this was Becky Friessen, Neil's mother, a woman who'd been nothing but kind and considerate and a friend to her, so she'd packed alongside Neil and, with the kids, met Brad and Emily with their three and flew out of the small Grays Harbor airfield to catch a flight to Cancun. Now settled in business class on the packed flight, she took in Emily and Brad across the aisle, their three children seated behind them. It was the way they sat together: He was holding his wife close, his chin on top of her head, and they were just touching, sharing their sorrow. She could see how much they loved each other even in this stressful time.

Neil stretched his leg out in the aisle. Cat was between them and sound asleep, and Candy's arm was starting to ache from holding Michael for so long. She leaned forward and unsnapped her seat belt.

"What are you doing?" Neil asked. She could see his distraction, whether about her or his mother.

"I need to get up. Can you take Michael?"

Neil unbuckled his belt and stood up, taking the baby while Candy scooted out into the aisle of the commercial airliner and started to the bathroom. Just as she reached for the door, she noticed it was occupied. She looked back as Neil sat again, holding the baby. In a row of seats at the front, a young couple was chatting. She was startled when she realized Brad was watching her. Emily's head rested against his chest, and his hand was linked with hers. He kissed her head and whispered something, and she moved as he stood up.

He resembled Neil in so many ways, except Brad was a rancher, and he dressed always in faded jeans, cowboy boots, and some type of western shirt. He was the same height as her husband, with a similar sexy build, but she was positive his shoulders were broader. He touched the seats as he strode up the aisle to where she stood waiting for her turn to use the bathroom. He stopped and rested his hand on the wall beside her, blocking her from Neil's view. Maybe that was why she let out a breath that sounded like relief.

"How are you doing?" he asked.

Brad was handsome, and right now she envied Emily for what she had with Brad. He was the eldest brother, and, to her, Brad seemed so together, so much in charge, the one who was there for everyone. It seemed so, anyway, to her.

"I should be asking you how you are," Candy said. "This is your mom. I can't imagine what this must be doing to you."

Brad blinked and looked away for a minute. Maybe she'd caught him off guard, as he didn't like talking about his feelings. But then, how many men did? Neil certainly didn't. "Not a great Christmas, that's for sure. There isn't much that can be done right now, though."

"Did you hear anything more about how she's doing?"

Brad shook his head. "No, same as you. She's in the ICU. Dad found her passed out in the bathroom. I'll call again when we land."

Candy nodded, her arms crossed in front of her. She was so tempted to reach out and touch Brad, but the confidence she had begun to cultivate had once again shattered. She needed time to find her feet again.

"I was planning on talking to you when we came over, before we got the news on Mom." Brad cleared his throat. "I got a call from a friend of mine that you went to see him."

Candy could feel the heat flood her cheeks. She already knew who he was talking about. "So who is this friend?" she asked, and Brad glanced away for a second. It was something he did when he was thinking of what to say, and it was so much like Neil. Did he have any idea how unnerving it was?

"Come on, you know who the friend is. Keith's a family friend, Candy. We went to school together. We're close. He didn't tell me details because he can't, and he wouldn't betray his client. Although he said you haven't retained him yet, he indicated you might. Are you planning on leaving my brother?"

She couldn't believe he'd asked that. She didn't know the answer herself. "Did you tell Neil?"

This time, he reached out and touched her shoulder, squeezing gently. "No, I did not tell Neil. You two have enough problems, enough you need to work through. But I worry, Candy. You going to a lawyer instead of working this out with my brother … it's not the answer, especially right now."

"Really? Your brother lied to me. How can I be married to a man I can't trust?"

"I'm not excusing what he did. There are no excuses, so let's just take that off the table. But there's a bigger picture you need to look at. You have two kids, you have an adoption that isn't even finalized, and you're in the middle of relocating. You're trying to keep so many balls in the air that you can't be thinking straight." He kept his voice low, but she wondered if anyone was picking up on the energy between them. It was tense, and she resented what Brad was implicating.

"You're making me sound selfish, as if I'm not thinking of my kids. I went to see Keith to find out my options. I can't believe he called you, that he told you," she snapped. She felt betrayed. Why couldn't anyone honor and respect her confidentiality? She hadn't paid him, as it had just been a consultation, but she was pretty sure she was protected by lawyer–client confidentiality. "He shouldn't have called you. That was wrong."

"Maybe so. I know he didn't want to, but he knows us. Whatever you told him bothered him enough that he asked me to talk to you. He didn't give me your details, but he didn't have to."

"Brad, I don't know what I'm going to do. Your brother hurt me badly, and if we didn't have Cat and Michael, I would be gone. I am thinking of them." She didn't say how heartbroken Cat would be if Neil wasn't there—or the fact that Neil would have once abandoned Cat to rot in an orphanage. Right now was the first time Cat had ever had stability, and that was the only reason Candy hadn't pushed and demanded Neil leave.

"Candy, being single without kids is a different story,

but with kids, you have more to think of, including what's best for them. I know that, Candy. There's no excuse for what Neil did. Let's just be clear, that was wrong, and you have every right to feel hurt and betrayed. I've been there. I had that in my life with my first wife, Crystal. She was a deceitful, callous woman who only thought of herself. My brother isn't that way, though. Whatever misguided notions had him making the stupid decision to create this lie, there's a big difference between my ex-wife and Neil.

"I've never seen my brother so torn up as he was when you found out what he did. He believed this was the only way to save his family, his marriage. He thought he was going to lose you, and having another man who was in love with you confront him, to have that man tell him you'd been confiding in him ..." Brad shook his head. Candy was stunned, and it took her a minute to recall Jim Miller, the pediatrician in Mexico, a handsome man who'd helped her with Cat. They had been friends, nothing more—in her mind, anyway. But she had confided in him when Neil had pulled away, giving all his attention to Maria, the surrogate, the woman who had given birth to Michael.

"There was nothing going on between me and Jim," Candy said. "He was a friend, that's all. He helped with Cat." He also wanted her, she knew that. She wasn't a fool. She didn't want to admit how far it had gone, though, or remember Jim's interest in her. He wanted more than friendship, and she hadn't been able to cross that line.

Brad was watching her closely. Maybe he could tell that she, too, had secrets. "Candy, you simply can't be friends with a man other than your husband. It can't happen. Lines become blurred more times than they not. Neil was jealous. I'd have been jealous, too. I probably would have killed him."

She didn't expect that from Brad. Maybe the shock in

her expression gave away what she was thinking, but Brad suddenly had a crazy alpha look about him as he watched her.

"Yes, Candy, there are some lines you don't cross. Were you considering leaving with this man, or was it truly innocent?"

She could say the same about Neil with Maria, and she was about to say something when Brad touched her shoulder again. "You're family, honey, but we don't have cheaters in the family. Take a step back, Candy, and take a really hard look at everything that happened to bring you here. I know you're considering leaving Neil, but this isn't the time. I think you know that. You still have work to do before you do something that can't be undone."

For a minute, she felt as if she'd done something wrong. Then Brad squeezed her shoulder again supportively, and something about it helped. "I would never cheat on Neil," she said. "I hope you know that. For a while, though, it felt as if he was cheating on me with Maria."

"Just promise me you won't leave or do anything else until you've talked to me?"

She wondered why Brad would say that. She nodded. "And you won't tell Neil?"

"As long as you talk to me, it will go no further, but I want your word, Candy. I saw that spooked look in your eyes, for a moment, like a horse who wants to run. Stay put. You talk to Neil, put effort into it. You have two kids you have to consider first. Think about what this would do to them."

The lock clicked, and the bathroom door opened. A man stepped out. She touched the edge of the door and glanced back at Brad, who was still close to her. "And if I can't stay with him?"

"You're family, Candy. No matter what happens, we look after family. Do you understand?"

Yeah, she understood. No slipping away, no hiding, but she also realized that somehow, someway, Brad would have her back.

Brad started back to his seat, and there was Neil, holding Michael, watching her.

Chapter 14

"Em, I'm sending you and the kids to Mom and Dad's to get settled," Brad said. "Ana and her husband, Carlos, will be there to help you. Neil and I are going to ride over to the hospital. I don't want the kids there until I know what's going on." He slid his arm around Emily and pulled her to him. Her hands slipped around his waist, and she pressed a kiss to his chest, then smoothed her hand over his dark shirt.

"All right, if that will help you," she replied. She was tired from the trip, but then, no one had slept since Rodney had phoned, sounding panicked about their mom. Brad had taken the phone from Neil and talked to his dad, and the only thing that had put the fear of God into him was when Rodney had said, "It doesn't look good." Maybe Emily knew that, because he had only shaken his head when the kids started crying about Grandma. "I'll take the kids, but I want to come to the hospital, Brad. You shouldn't be there alone."

"I'm not alone, but I need to see what's going on first."

He saw two of their four suitcases slide down the conveyor belt, and he reached for them and lifted them onto the cart. "Trevor, Katy, Becky, stay here with your mom."

"When can we see Grandma?" Becky asked, holding the hand of her twelve-year-old half-sister, Katy. Katy had really light hair tied back in a ponytail, and Becky's hair was darker, shoulder length, sticking up in places. They were holding their jackets, wearing jeans, T-shirts, and sneakers, and Trevor was standing with his hands behind his back, watching the suitcases go by.

"Is that ours, Dad?" Trevor asked as he pointed at one of their red suitcases. He was getting so big.

"Yes, it is. Grab it, Trevor."

"Brad, I think that's the last one." Emily pointed to a suitcase with a missing wheel, which had fallen off in Seattle.

He tossed it onto the cart as Emily herded the kids together and toward the door. Brad called out to Neil, who had already claimed their luggage. Candy was holding the baby, and Neil had tossed Cat on top of the cart and was holding her while he pushed. She seemed to like that.

"I'm sending Em and the kids to the estate from here," Brad said. "You and I can grab a cab." He glanced to Candy.

"I'll go back to the house with Emily," she said. "Michael needs to be changed and fed."

There was still tension between Candy and Neil, and the distance between them was huge. Anyone could see, as they walked out of the airport, that they were one very unhappy couple. Brad helped Neil load all the bags in the trunk of the black limo, the one Neil had called ahead for, the one from his resort.

Brad kissed Emily, and he could see how Neil stood

back and just watched as Candy climbed in. He didn't try to touch her, but he did kiss Cat and help her in. Brad couldn't do anything for them. He was so worried about his mother, and it was killing him trying to hold everyone together while at the same time trying to get to the hospital as soon as he could.

"I'll get us a cab," Neil said as Brad leaned inside, seeing everyone piled in the back of the limo.

"I'll call you from the hospital," he said. "Jed and Diana are on their way, too."

Emily reached for Brad's arm. "I love you. Call me. We'd like to be there. The kids need to know."

He knew what she was saying, and he could see the worry on the kids' faces, but the last thing he wanted was his kids sitting around a hospital waiting room. It would be better if they weren't there. He could protect them from that. "Stay put until I call you," he said, and he knew Emily wanted to disagree, but she just touched his hand again.

"Call as soon as you get there, just to let me know, even if there's no news."

He nodded and then took in Candy, whose expression was guarded. Then he shut the door and tapped the hood for the driver to take his family to the estate. He stood there for a moment in the bright sunshine, watching.

"Brad," Neil called, holding open the door of a cab. "Let's go."

Brad climbed in the backseat beside Neil and had just closed the door when the cab driver pulled away.

"Jed sent a text—or rather, Diana did it for him. Their flight has been delayed, but they're hoping to leave in an hour. Of all the times for this to happen. Did you hear from Dad again?" Neil asked. He sounded agitated and was rambling. "Step on it, would you?" He tapped the back of the cabby's seat.

"No, I just left Dad a message that we'd landed and you and I are coming to the hospital."

Brad watched as Neil wiped his face with his hand and glanced out the side window. Was he even listening? With his marriage one step from the toilet, along with their mother now in the hospital, this was the first time Brad had seen Neil so scattered. But then, everyone had a breaking point.

It didn't take long to pull up in front of the hospital. It was larger than Brad thought it would be, four stories, with large glass front doors. Brad pulled out American dollars from his wallet and handed them to the cabby.

Neil was through the front doors of the hospital before Brad and was standing at the information desk. "My mother was brought in. She had a stroke. Becky Friessen is her name. Can you tell me where she is?" he asked.

The woman behind the desk typed into the computer and said, "She's in intensive care. Only family is allowed."

"She's my mother, too," Brad said.

"Third floor." She pointed to a set of elevators. Brad put his hand on Neil's shoulder, and they walked to the elevator. Neil pressed the button twice, then jabbed it a few more times when it didn't open.

"It's not gonna get here any quicker, Neil."

"Maybe I'll take the stairs." Neil took a step and turned, looking for the door, when the elevator dinged and several people stepped out. Brad followed Neil in, and an orderly with someone in a wheelchair also followed them. When Brad leaned over and held the door for them, he didn't miss Neil's annoyance. He sighed, and as soon as they cleared the door, Neil jammed the button for the third floor. The orderly pressed two, and Neil sighed again.

The door opened, the orderly pushed the patient out of the elevator, and Neil was jabbing the button to close the doors.

"You okay?" Brad said.

"Yeah, fine," he snapped. When the doors opened and they stepped into the hallway, there was glass everywhere, reflecting doctors, nurses, and hospital personnel.

"Neil." Brad tapped his brother's arm when he spotted open doors and a station where all the personnel seemed to be coming and going.

Neil was ahead of him, and Brad could feel his chest tightening. Maybe it was the sterile hospital smell, the disinfectant, the machines beeping, the phones ringing. It was active and buzzing.

"Excuse me, we're looking for my mother, Becky Friessen. She was brought in after a stroke," Neil said, tapping the counter. A man with dark hair was scribbling something in a chart, and he didn't look up. There was another woman behind the counter, and she gestured to the man with her.

"Dr. Cortes, that's your patient, isn't it?" she asked. The lady was a doctor or a nurse. Brad couldn't tell the difference, as they were both in scrubs.

"Yes, she is." He spoke in clipped tones and then closed up the chart and slid it in a rack with several others, flicking his pen closed. "Donna, check on Mr. Taylor in four. Let me know when his labs are back. Is the family still here?"

"In the waiting room, his sister and a daughter," the woman said, pointing down the hall.

"Okay, I'll need to talk to them. Excuse me." He glanced over at Brad and Neil and started to walk away as if dismissing them, then stopped. "My intern here will take you in to see your mother, but don't stay long."

"Whoa, wait a second," Neil said. "How is our mother? Is my dad still here? Can't you tell us anything?" He took a step toward the doctor, who was walking away.

"I will come back and find you, but I have other patients and something else I need to deal with." The doctor was close to their height and appeared closer to their age—young. He stepped toward Neil and touched his shoulder. "Go see your mother. I'll see you and speak with you as soon as I can." This time, the doctor looked them both in the eye for a second. He had deep blue eyes. Then he was gone, hurrying down the hall.

"Your mother is in the first bed," the intern said. "Your father has been here all night and stayed with her after she came out of surgery."

"She had surgery?" Brad asked, following her into an ICU with several beds, machines, and tubes. There was his mother, lying in a bed, covered with a white sheet, hooked up to a respirator. There was a white bandage around her head, and his father was slumped in the chair beside her.

"Mr. Friessen." The intern touched his father's shoulder. Rodney blinked and then sat up when he saw Neil and Brad.

"You're here." He cleared his throat.

"How's Mom doing? She had surgery?" Brad asked, standing at the foot of the bed. He noticed how Neil was beside the bed, his hand covering their mom's frail one.

"The doctor rushed her …" Rodney started to say. He glanced to the intern.

"Your mother suffered a stroke, a massive brain bleed, and the only way to stop it was to clip the aneurism. The doctor will explain everything when he comes to talk to you." She stepped around the chair and was shining a light in their mom's eyes. Then she pushed some buttons on the machine his mom was hooked up to.

It was horrible, watching her like this. Becky had held them all together, and now his mom, who should have been enjoying all the things retired folks did, was lying there in critical condition. Seeing her like this, Brad realized it was worse than he'd imagined.

Chapter 15

"I'm not about to give you false hope about your mother," Dr. Cortes said. "With stroke victims, time is of the essence. Every second a decision isn't made works against your mother. Your father thought quickly, calling for help, and the ambulance driver and paramedics knew that stopping at the wrong hospital meant life or death for your mom. They got her here. We're the only hospital in Mexico with a department specializing in strokes. Your mom had a massive brain bleed. That's why she passed out. She would have had symptoms days, weeks before—dizziness, headaches, confusion, slurred speech. The fact she's here at this hospital is the only reason she's still alive."

Neil was standing beside Brad, their father between them. Neil thought this doctor had an arrogance he'd never heard before. "So you're saying you're the best in this field?" he said. Why the hell did it sound like he was challenging him? Maybe because Neil hated false confidence, and if this guy thought he was good, he had to be the best.

"Yes, as a matter of fact, I am," Cortes replied. "Now, the fact that your mother hasn't woken up can mean many things. We won't know the extent of the damage until she does wake up."

"You mean *if* she wakes up," Neil snapped.

"Neil, let the doctor finish," Brad said.

"I want to know my wife's chances," Rodney interjected. "You promised you wouldn't give us false hope. Tell me what you do know."

The doctor reached out and touched Rodney's shoulder. "Mr. Friessen, as much as we know about the brain, it is still a mystery. All we can do now is take it one day at a time. Your wife is still here. She made it through the night. If your family is all here, you need to bring them in to see her."

"Is my wife going to make it?" Rodney asked. It was first time Neil had heard his dad sounding as if something was breaking inside him.

"Her chances aren't good. She has a ten percent chance only, based on the type of stroke she had. Is there no hope? Absolutely not. There's always hope. However, you need to prepare yourself for the worst, and your family, too. I'll be back to check on her." The doctor walked away, and Neil watched as his dad seemed to sag. Brad grabbed his arm.

"Dad, come and sit down." He led him over to a chair in the waiting area, which was now empty.

"Your mother never said anything," Rodney said. "Yes, she's been forgetful lately. I know this week she was doing some odd things. She was confused. I just thought she was doing too much. She's always had so much on her mind, always worrying about one of you. You know, we were getting ready to go see Diana and Jed for Christmas this year. I didn't know something was wrong. She said she was fine. I thought she was …" Rodney glanced up at Neil as he stood in front of his dad.

He knew what his dad was saying. His mom was worried about him, about what he'd done.

"Dad," Jed called out as he hurried in. He looked a mess, his hair sticking up as if he'd run his fingers through it, a five o'clock shadow on his cheeks as if he hadn't shaved in a few days. He wore a faded green T-shirt and what Neil thought was his oldest pair of blue jeans. Diana, his redheaded wife, was holding his hand, looking neat and tidy in a pair of cream-colored slacks and a black T-shirt. "How's Mom doing?" Jed asked. He hugged Neil and Brad, then his dad.

Diana followed, and she touched Neil's arm. "Hey."

He had forgotten how blue her eyes were, how deep her smile was. He had forgotten the sadness he knew would always be a part of her. Brad kissed her cheek, and then she reached up and slid her arms around Neil, and he was forced to hug her. If she only knew what he'd done, would she still hug him so freely? She pulled back and looked at him, narrowing her eyes as if trying to figure him out. She patted his arm. "Good to see you, Neil. Brad, you too. I wish it were under happier circumstances."

Jed slid his arm around Diana, pulled her against him, and kissed the top of her head. "We dropped Danny and Christopher off at the estate with Laura. Everyone's here."

"Hi," Andy said as he strode in. He had short dark hair, icy blue eyes, and wore black jeans and a blue dress shirt with an open collar. "Laura and I ran into Jed and Diana at the airport."

Neil hadn't expected Andy, his cousin, to come, too.

"Any news?" Andy asked, looking first at Rodney, who was shaking his head, and then to Neil. He touched his arm. "It's good to see you. I had a chance to see Candy and the baby for a second before we left, and that little girl you adopted." He didn't say anything else, but Neil wondered. He hadn't spoken to Andy or Jed about the situation, but he could feel Jed watching him, too, for a second. How would they know anything about what he'd done? Brad did, and so did his dad, but he didn't expect either to have shared it.

"We're in a waiting game right now. The doctor wants us to have everyone come in and see Mom," Brad said. He cleared his throat, his voice sounding thick. He didn't look up, but he didn't need to for Neil to see that his eyes were misty. He knew his own were. He'd been fighting the urge to slip away alone.

Maybe Andy knew, as he put his hand on his shoulder and squeezed.

"I'm going to get Em and the kids, bring them up," Brad said.

Jed was still holding Diana. "Diana and I are going to go in and see Mom."

"I'm going back in, as well," Rodney said, and he started toward the ICU, Diana and Jed with him.

Brad turned to Neil. "You coming? You should bring Candy in."

Neil could feel his brother watching him, and maybe Andy had picked up on something, after all, as he was watching closely, too, as if he'd figured out something was going on. "You go," Neil said. "I'm going to stay."

Maybe Brad had decided not to push, as he nodded and then walked away, leaving Neil alone with Andy.

Chapter 16

Candy hadn't realized how much she missed her room, their bedroom. Everything was still the same, the four-poster, the gold comforter, the red area rug, and the mahogany dresser, makeup stand, and side tables. It was a large room, very comfortable, and so was the amazing bathroom with the sunken tub and the shower so big she could walk around in it. She missed all of it, but then she felt the remembered ache of when Maria had been across the hall in the spare bedroom. She could still see it in her mind, and for a second it nearly took her breath away. But now it was Cat and Becky who were staying in there, and a crib had been set up in the corner for Michael, who was sleeping soundly. There was so much that hadn't changed, but at the same time, there was so much that had.

Most of her clothes were still here. Neil's, too. She took in the racks of unworn dresses, suits, dress shirts, shoes. She supposed Neil had planned to pack up and ship all of this to their new home, Neil's new house, the one she lived in with so much uncertainty. What would happen now?

She changed into one of her long cotton skirts and pulled on a peach, cap-sleeved T-shirt, then slipped her bare feet into a pair of her old sandals, which had been shoved into the back of the closet. She couldn't help smiling when she thought of Neil's reaction. He'd bought her two new pairs of sandals to replace the old ones, telling her to throw them out, but she wasn't like Neil. She didn't need flash and glitter and nice things. This was Neil's world, a world he'd tried to fit her into, a world that was suddenly gone with all the changes he would have to make. They were broke, he needed to sell the resort, and he'd paid Maria five million dollars for Michael.

She lowered her head in her hands. "Oh, Neil, why?" she whispered. It was a mess, all of it. The woman hadn't gone away. She was still a thorn in their side, doing whatever she could to destroy their happiness. Candy hated Maria, and even though she wanted to hate Neil, she couldn't. She loved him, but the hurt he'd caused, and the deceit, the lies that he'd brought into their life, she knew she couldn't live with that.

She rubbed lotion on her hands and brushed her freshly washed hair, then picked up the baby monitor as she pulled open the bedroom door. Upstairs, it was quiet, and she couldn't hear the kids. There were Brad and Emily's three, and Jed and Diana had stopped by long enough to drop off Danny and Christopher, a handful at ages four and two. Then there were Andy and Laura's three. Gabriel looked good playing with all the kids outside in the backyard. He'd had no relapse in his leukemia and was now thriving like all the other kids.

The estate was mayhem. Even though it was large enough for the entire family, there were kids everywhere, and the energy was all over the place. It had to be the anxiety, the traveling, and the fact that Christmas was now on hold that had all the kids on short fuses. Trevor was bouncing on the sofa alone. Great!

"Trevor, why don't you play with your sisters and Cat outside?" Candy said.

"No, it's fine." He actually waved his hand and then lay on the sofa. "I'm going to take a nap."

"Okay," Candy replied. She didn't know what to do, but she was sure that if Emily had been on top of things, she would have been all over Trevor, sending him to play with the other kids. But she wasn't, because she was on the phone in the kitchen, pacing. Laura was there, too, with the twins, who were now walking and into everything. At almost two, Chelsea and Jeremy were a handful. Jeremy pulled, threw, and stomped, and his sister sat and played. Candy had to smile, because even as babies, Jeremy had been the demanding one and Chelsea the angel.

"Ana, I put Michael in his crib," Candy said as she caught sight of the housekeeper. "He's asleep. Oh, and please thank your husband for setting it up."

Ana had dark hair woven with a lot of gray. She was short and plump, and she was pulling food out of the fridge and making sandwiches. "We were so excited that you were coming back, you and Neil, and bringing the baby and the little girl. We're just so sorry it had to be like this." She cried out the last part, and a tear slipped out. "I'm sorry." She wiped her face.

"Oh, no, I'm sorry. This has to be even harder on you. You've known Becky longer," Candy said.

"Mrs. Friessen is such a good, kind woman," Ana said. Candy rubbed her shoulder and put the baby monitor on the counter. Ana reached up and patted Candy's hand.

"Brad's not answering," Emily said. "He must have his phone turned off. I asked him to call to let me know, and he still hasn't." She seemed distracted and tense as she put the phone down and touched her forehead.

Laura glanced over a little apprehensively and then to Candy. Her blond hair was past her shoulders, and her cheeks were fuller than Candy remembered. She had filled out and wasn't quite as thin as she had been, even though she still had a great figure. And she was still so shy.

"Has Neil called you?" Emily asked, putting her hand at her throat. Her voice sounded strained.

"No." She shook her head. "My SUV—I mean, Neil's SUV is still here. It think it is." Or maybe Neil had already sold it. She didn't know.

"Both yours and Mr. Neil's are here, parked by the garage," Ana said. "Keys are in the drawer by the fridge." She pulled herself together, wiped her nose, and then washed her hands under the tap.

"Emily, I just want to check on my horse and donkey, and then I could drive us to the hospital. Ana, would you be okay here with the kids?" Maybe she was asking too much. Ana was cooking for everyone, and she, too, was worried about Becky. But then, Katy was old enough to help, and Cat was so happy with her cousins. She was sure they'd be okay.

"If you two go, I'll help Ana with the kids," Laura said as she picked up Jeremy, who was reaching for a placemat stacked neatly on the table. "I don't think so, buddy," she said as she lifted him and stumbled a bit. Her face was flushed.

"Are you okay, Laura?" Candy asked. Then Emily was there, reaching for her arm and taking Jeremy from her. The boy was all smiles and dark hair, and anyone could see he was looking for trouble.

"Just dizzy for a minute," Laura said. She blushed and

then smiled. "This is probably not the time, but I'm pregnant again."

"Oh, that's wonderful!" Emily said.

"You should sit down, then," Ana added, and she started to fuss over Laura, who just shook her head and said, "I'm fine, really. I'd been sitting for so long on the plane, and someone has to run after this guy." Then Chelsea got up from where she was stacking colorful plastic blocks under the table and ran to Laura. "And you, you're the easy one until you want me." Laura kissed her plump-cheeked daughter, who was patting her face.

"Laura, I'm really happy for you if this is what you wanted. Andy's not giving you much of a break," Candy said. She couldn't believe the words had left her mouth.

Even Emily gave her an odd look. Laura appeared ashamed for a moment, and that was the last thing Candy wanted her to feel. After everything, she'd pulled her life together from being an unwed teenage mother with Gabriel. Candy was making a mess of this all because she was angry at Neil. "I'm sorry, Laura. That wasn't what I meant."

"Andy wants a big family," Laura said. "He was an only child, and he doesn't want that for our kids. I love my life with Andy and the kids, and I wouldn't trade it. Being a mother is the one thing I'm really good at."

Candy couldn't remember Laura ever speaking with such confidence.

The front door closed. "Dad, you're back," Trevor called out, and Candy could hear Brad saying something to him.

"It's about time he's back." Emily sounded irritated as she handed Jeremy to Ana and patted his back before starting out of the kitchen, but she stopped as Brad walked in alone. He appeared tense, and he took in everyone at the same time. He was distracted as he put his hands on Emily.

"We need to take the kids up to the hospital." He didn't say anything else, but Candy understood what he was saying. Maybe Emily did, too.

"Oh, Brad, no." She wrapped her arms around him and buried her face in his chest.

"It's going to be okay." Brad's voice was rough, and it was the first time Candy thought Brad would cry. He hadn't ever cried, she thought.

"Brad, how is Becky? And Neil, is he …" She wanted to ask if her husband was okay. No matter where they were, this had to be killing him.

"He stayed at the hospital. Andy's with him, and Jed and Diana went in to see Mom. Candy, you should come. Mom's …" He cleared his throat and couldn't finish the sentence. He was still holding Emily as he said it, and he was watching her in that way of his. She knew there had to be so much more he wasn't saying. This was his way of protecting his family, a man with such broad shoulders to carry the weight of it. But there was a cold reality he couldn't protect any of them from.

"How bad is it, Brad?" She pressed her hand to her throat and realized it was shaking. Why was she trembling? It wasn't as if Becky was her mother. She was Neil's, but, then, she'd always been there for Candy. She'd never once taken Neil's side over hers. Becky Friessen didn't take sides. She never overstepped her boundaries, either. She never pushed Candy. Why hadn't Neil come home, too? She wished Neil were here now. Right now, in this moment, she felt alone in a way she hadn't in so long. She ached, realizing it was a place she didn't want to go back to.

"Bad," he said. "She may not make it. You need to

prepare for that, and you need to say goodbye in case. Candy, you need to come back with us."

She nodded as she felt herself choking on a sob. She wiped her face and then pressed her hands together. "You go. I'm going to see Sable and Ambrose. I haven't seen them yet. They probably need some hay, some exercise, and I need to make sure they're okay. You go ..." She didn't know what she was saying as she backed up and tripped over a stool Jeremy had slid across the room. She stumbled and then righted herself, sliding her hand on the wall and slipping toward the door. She pulled it open and realized everyone was quiet and watching. Maybe they thought she'd lost her mind. "I'm sorry. Ana, please, can you watch my kids? I—I've got to go out ..." She couldn't finish as she stepped outside into the setting sun, pulling the door closed so they couldn't see her, and then she started to run.

Chapter 17

"Neil, she's freaking out. You have to go and talk to her. I don't think she's going to come, and she shouldn't be driving, anyway," Brad said. He was standing with Emily, his arm around her in the waiting room. Katy and little Becky were sitting with their grandfather, who'd just come out of Becky's room. The doctor had sent everyone out so he could examine her. He told them to have a seat and he would come out and speak with them.

"What's going on?" Jed asked. Diana, whose eyes were red, slid her hand over his arm.

Andy was squatting in front of the kids and Rodney, talking to them. Whatever he was saying seemed to reassure the kids, at least.

Brad was now shaking his head, and everyone had to know how disappointed he was in him, but Neil also knew Brad wouldn't say anything.

"I don't think this is really the time," he said, hoping Jed wouldn't ask any more. Then Andy stepped into their circle beside Emily, taking in everyone.

"What's going on?" he asked.

"Neil has a problem with Candy," Jed said. "All I know is that she's at home, upset, and won't come to the hospital. What I don't understand, Neil, is why you aren't going to get her."

Andy now crossed his arms, watching Neil with his dark, brooding look.

Out of everyone, Neil knew his cousin understood him better than his brothers. "I don't think Candy wants me coming to get her. I guarantee you I'm the last person she wants to see," he snapped in a low voice, hoping the kids were far enough away that they couldn't hear him.

Jed and Diana exchanged a confused look, and Andy was waiting for him to finish.

"What's going on, Neil?" Jed asked. "You just moved across the country. You're not even settled yet, with a baby and a little girl. Did something happen?" He was pushing, and he even took a step closer and glanced over at his dad. "Neil, she's your wife. You have to go get her. Whatever's going on between you two, you need to put it aside." Jed wasn't the brother who pushed—that was Brad—but maybe the fact that he was out of loop, that they hadn't talked in so long, had him taking this stand.

"It's not that simple, Jed. I did something she may never forgive me for."

He didn't miss the sorrow on Emily's face, and he could tell Brad agreed with him. At the same time, he hoped someone would tell him it wasn't that bad. He knew it was worse.

"What the hell did you do, cheat on your wife?" Jed snapped, and Diana elbowed him, but he could see how she was thinking the same thing. He didn't want to see that disappointment on the faces of his family.

"I lied to Candy about the baby. I was so afraid of losing her because of Cat, the little girl we adopted."

"The deaf girl?" Jed said, and Diana elbowed him again.

"Yes, the deaf girl Candy found in an orphanage. I didn't want her. I wanted a baby, and I did everything to make it happen. I went too far with the surrogate, Maria, and didn't see how Candy was being pushed out, so I told her Maria lost the baby, and I pushed them to the back of my mind when we left for Arizona. I put everything into helping Cat, and when the baby was born, I paid Maria five million to sign away her rights and leave us alone."

Shock didn't quite describe the expressions on Jed and Diana's faces. Even Andy wore a look of disbelief. Jed started to say something and then let out a sharp breath. "Seriously?" He was shaking his head.

"Neil ..." Diana started to say. He felt horrible in that moment, seeing disappointment on her face. She, of all his family, he never wanted to disappoint. She was the one he had promised to take care of if anything happened to Jed. He had a soft spot for her. She'd had a hard life before Jed.

"All I can say is that I'm sorry," Neil said. "I never wanted Candy to find out, and instead of telling her the truth, I just kept on lying. I told her a baby had just conveniently come available, and I would have moved my family to the other side of the world if it meant she'd never find out. But Maria wouldn't let it go. She kept calling my cell phone, so I changed the number. Somehow she found us and sent a letter. And, as the story goes, my wife read it, so now you know why I can't go and get her. She hates me and is only here now because of Mom. She doesn't want me around her."

Andy rubbed both hands over his face. Even after every bad thing he'd done—and Andy could be a real asshole when he wanted to—he appeared stunned. Jed was rubbing the back of his neck, but Diana, the way she watched him … something in her expression softened.

"Oh, Neil, I'm so sorry." She actually reached out and touched his arm. "It seems that the men in this family love to keep secrets." She glanced up at her husband.

"Diana, that was different. I was trying to protect you, and it's my job to look after you and the kids." Jed sounded defensive, but, then, it was true that he'd once hidden his dire financial straits from Diana, only letting her find out how bad things were after an accident threatened his life.

Diana actually rolled her eyes. "I'm capable, Jed. You know that. I know how to stand on my own two feet. Got a law degree to prove it."

"But you shouldn't have to. Besides, that's water under the bridge, Diana," Jed said, and Neil didn't miss the shared moment between Emily and Brad, either, the way he seemed to tighten his hold on her.

"Neil, you need to go home and talk to Candy," Diana said. "Whatever you did is done. Candy's reasonable, maybe in shock, still, but this is a time you should be together. I don't know how I would feel in Candy's place, truly, but I do know you can't leave her alone now. We all need to be here." Maybe Diana understood that better than anyone.

"I don't think she'll talk to me. You don't know how angry she is."

"I think Diana's right," Brad said. "She's angry. She has every right to be, Neil. We warned you it would be better coming from you."

"You know what, Brad?" Neil said. "Would you stop the nagging? It's getting old. I can't go back and change what I did. I wish I could, and let me remind you that you've done your share of hurtful things to Emily."

"Hey, you two, stop it," Andy snapped. "Neil, you're right. You can't go back. We all have things we've done in our pasts that we wish we could go back and undo, but this isn't the time for the blame game, who did the worst, most horrible thing."

Diana's gaze landed on Andy. Neil knew enough about their past to know that it was so dark and twisted, filled with such pain, because of Andy's father—their uncle, Todd—a man so different from Rodney that Neil often wondered how they could be family.

Maybe he needed to get out of here, take a breath. "Fine, I'll go," he said. He just hoped Candy would listen, that they weren't so far gone that he couldn't reason with her.

He walked away but stopped at his dad. Rodney didn't look up right away, but what Neil saw on his dad's face was loss. His dad was the head of the family, a man who spoke his mind when needed, and he'd always been there for all of them. "Dad, I'm going home to get Candy," he finally said.

His father only nodded. "I'm going to check to see if the doctor's done," he said, and he pushed out of the chair, his light pants wrinkled. For the first time ever, Neil saw a five o'clock shadow on his father's face, and he was about to ask if he wanted to come home to shower and change, but he realized there was no way he was going to leave their mother.

Neil started to the elevator.

"Neil, wait up," Andy called out and started toward him. "I'll come with you. It will give me a chance to check on Laura and the kids." Neil pressed the button and noticed Andy glance back at everyone. When the elevator door opened, it was crammed with passengers, and they stepped in and rode down. The elevator emptied, and Neil, with Andy beside him and without saying a word, walked outside to where a cab was waiting.

"I wanted to talk to you about this problem you have," Andy said.

Andy held open the back door. Neil climbed in and gave the address to the driver. "I'll grab my SUV and drive it back to the hospital so we're not paying for cabs to go back and forth," he said. He didn't want to talk any more about what he'd done.

"You surprise the hell out of me sometimes, Neil."

"Look, if you're about to tell me how stupid I am for lying to my wife, for not coming clean, I've already heard it from Dad and from Brad. I don't want to hear it from you, too. I know I should have told her."

"Hey, look, I'm not about to come down on you. This is me. But, fuck, Neil, you paid the broad five million. Of anyone, I would have thought you had the best business sense. That was …" Andy ran his hand over his jaw as if he was thinking of what else to say.

"Stupid? Is that what you were going to say? And desperate? I was. I did one of the dumbest things ever because I was so blinded by my need to have a baby, to have a family. I let my better judgment take a backseat. Even my wife tried to warn me, but I wouldn't listen to her, and I ignored what it was doing to her. She can't ever have children, and maybe I'll never get past her losing the baby. Maybe I'll never forgive her for ignoring her symptoms and not saying anything to me and damn near dying.

"Maybe I was still angry about it when I pushed for a surrogate, and then I kept pushing Maria in her face, and Maria kept changing things, and I went along with it, and the distance between Candy and me grew. But you know what, Andy? This personal thing … having a surrogate carry your baby is a business decision, but the lines became blurred. I've never allowed business to cross into my personal life. I've always made sure contracts are signed and whatever deal I'm making is in my favor, but this was different. It was my child."

"Look, I can't pretend to understand what you and Candy have. I know how you felt when Candy had the hysterectomy to save her life. I know what you went through. Honestly, Neil, I thought you two were done then."

Of course he didn't like what Andy was saying, and he wanted to jump in and defend his wife, but Andy stopped him.

"Look, Neil, nothing here is straightforward. I like Candy. When you two showed up to help me and Laura with the twins and helped us hold it together when Gabriel was so sick …" He glanced away and swallowed, and Neil wondered for a moment if everything was okay.

"Is Gabriel okay? I should have asked how he's doing. Any relapse?"

Andy shook his head. "No, no, Gabriel's fine. Doing better than I expected. He just had his yearly follow-up, and there are no signs of a relapse. It's just that I always worry, and I wonder if it will forever be in the back of my mind how close we came to losing Gabriel. The adoption's final, you know. Gabriel is mine." Andy was smiling as he glanced over at Neil again. "So I was really surprised when I heard you'd adopted a little deaf girl, because you told me once that adoption wasn't for you."

He had said that, he realized. He'd said a lot of things he didn't believe anymore. "I never expected to fall in love with Cat the way I did. I can't imagine not having her in my life. I was wrong about that."

"So let me get this straight: You have a little girl you

adopted, a wife you love, and a son who's yours. Don't you have everything you want?"

What the hell was Andy getting at? Of course this was everything he wanted. He had a family, a wife he loved, children he loved. He wanted nothing but a life with them, raising his children, loving his wife, and to have Maria out of their lives forever. "Of course, but that isn't the point."

"Well, actually, it is, Neil. You make your wife listen to you. You apologize. You make it up to her. And you make sure that, this time, you get everything in order. Because from where I'm sitting, it seems to me the only problem you have is a woman who won't go away."

Chapter 18

She stood at the edge of the fence separating her private beach from Neil's new resort, the spot where her house had once been. When that storm swept in, it had taken everything she had left. To her, this had been the biggest obstacle between her and Neil, and this piece of beach she walked Sable down now had been the one place she could come to be alone. She'd needed this piece of land, or so she thought, to keep herself centered, believing it was as much a part of her as she was of it.

But it didn't hold the same draw as it once had. Maybe that was from being away for so long. First in Arizona with Cat, and now up in Washington State, by Emily and Brad, with a baby, in a new home on an oceanfront acreage. She ran her hand over the smoky gray of Sable's neck and rested her arm over his back. He snorted but stood with her in the sand just a few feet from the lapping waves. She breathed in the salty air, waiting for that feeling she'd always gotten just from being here. But it didn't come, not this time, because her thoughts came drifting back to where her heart was, with her children, Cat and Michael.

Of course, separating Neil from that was about as difficult as not swallowing. She couldn't do it, because every time she saw the smile on her little girl's face, it was filled with joy because Neil was there, too.

"What am I going to do?" she asked Sable. She hated change, she always had. Maybe she just didn't realize now how much she needed to know everything was where it was supposed to be. But here they were with a new home in Washington, a move only half done, and her horse and donkey still here in Mexico. Could they move back here? No. They couldn't come back here, she realized as she climbed onto Sable's back and started back to the house, because her memories here were filled with a woman she despised, a woman who was the source of much of her misery now.

She couldn't stand to be this close to Maria, in a country that could, without a second's notice, take Michael from her. She felt panic whisper at her back, and she was nearly unseated from her horse when she realized the implications of being back in Mexico with a baby she thought of as hers. Then there was Becky. Candy was now suddenly torn between getting on the first plane back to the States to hide from Maria and rushing to the hospital to see her mother-in-law.

She didn't realize she was riding so fast as she broke into a canter, taking a trail along the side of the house back to the stable and corral where her donkey, Ambrose, was waiting. She pulled up and climbed down, her legs shaking when a hand touched her back, her hips, and she turned around, gasping as her horse sidestepped, knocking her forward. She landed against Neil, his solid chest. His strong arms surrounded her. He was wearing the same dark shirt he'd worn on the plane, and she didn't miss the shadow on his face. He needed to shave.

"Are you all right?" he asked, looking down on her. This was the first time in so long that she'd been this close to him. She needed to move, but he was still holding on to her.

"Yes, I'm just …" She expected him to say something about her riding like a crazy person and racing her horse back here—riding in a skirt and sandals, too. He reached up to touch her cheek or brush her hair back, she wasn't sure which, but she turned her head away, and he dropped his hand.

"I was worried when I saw you race in here. I've never known you to ride Sable that hard."

She wanted to tell him why she was worried, but when she looked at him, all she could see was the heartache he was doing his best to hide from her. "How's your mom?" she asked, but she didn't think much had changed since Brad had been here, wanting them to come to the hospital. She knew he was trying to prepare her to say goodbye.

He just shook his head. His lips thinned as he blinked, and she didn't miss the sheen in his eyes. He breathed deeply. "She's not good, Candy. The doctor said she's maybe got a ten percent chance. He said we need to …" He shut his eyes again before looking at her. "You need to come and say goodbye to Mom."

She didn't want to hear this, and her heart ached as she realized how much her husband was hurting. "I'm so sorry, Neil. I know how much your mom means to all of you." Becky was a huge part of this family. She and Rodney were rocks everyone called on when needed.

"Mom admired you so much," he said. "Listen to me. I'm talking as if she's already gone." He shut his eyes again, and for a minute Candy thought her strong husband was going to fall apart.

It was instinctive to reach out and touch his arm. "Oh,

Neil, this isn't fair. Your mom is wonderful," she said. She was surprised to learn that Becky admired her, Candy, who was uneducated, klutzy, and almost inept, or at least had been in almost every social situation.

"I know this isn't the time to talk about us, but I need you to come to the hospital. Come back with me. Can you please just put aside your hate for me right now?"

She stepped away and tied her horse to the corral. "I don't hate you, Neil." She knew she was confused on her feelings. She had felt hatred for Neil at one time, but how could she hate a man she now loved so deeply? Everything about their relationship to this point had been filled with so much tragedy and heartache, though, and here they were with another obstacle of Neil's making.

"You know my dad was everything to me," Candy said, "and he filled my head with lies about you, that you wanted me only for our property. You know I believed him for so long, and it kept me away from you for how many years? Every time, then, when you asked me out, I said no." It had never made sense to Candy how her dad could say such things about Neil, the man who had risked his own life, when the hurricane swept through, to save her, who had stayed with her to keep her safe when she wouldn't leave her home or her animals. He had never taken her property from her after the bank took it away when she couldn't pay the bills. No, again she'd been wrong. Neil had given it back to her free and clear after he paid off the debt, and she was the one who had chosen to gift it to him so he could build the resort. She loved him, and he hadn't done what she believed he had. Neil Friessen may have been a lot of things, but he wasn't a monster.

Neil had an odd look on his face, and she wondered for a second if he was about to say something. Then he just looked away and started unsaddling her horse. "Why don't

I give you a hand here?" He stopped. "Is it all right if I help you?"

If the situation with his mom hadn't been sitting over them like a heavy blanket of darkness, she thought she might have smiled. "You're asking me if you can help me when you've always just stepped in and done it for me?" She'd meant to sound teasing, but she didn't think he'd taken it that way.

"I love you, and I only want to protect you from everything. That's why, I guess, I do what I do. I worry things will be hard for you."

"I'm not helpless, Neil," she said.

"I know you're not. You're strong and capable, and there are days I wished I had just an ounce of your empathy. You awe me with what you do."

What the hell was that? She just stared at her husband in disbelief until she realized he really meant what he'd said. "Why do you make me feel incapable, then? Like unsaddling Sable, I can do this myself. I've done it for years without you."

"I'm sorry, Candy. The last thing I intended you to feel is incapable, but I can't help it. I want to do everything I can to make your life easier."

"You do make my life easier. When you left, I found myself counting the minutes until you came back. You make me doubt what I can do by taking care of everything. I realized in the hours after you left how much I depend on you, and then I worried. If something happened to you, what would I do? I'm angry for thinking like that, because before there was you, I did everything myself. It wasn't easy, but I did it, and you make things so easy for me that when something comes along and rips the rug out from under me, I don't have my footing."

Neil didn't lift the saddle off for her. He actually

stepped back, giving her room as she lifted it off herself. It was a heavy western saddle, and for a second she almost dropped it. She could hear him without looking up, knowing he had to stop himself from reaching down and taking it from her. But she managed to carry it into the tack room. When she came out, Neil was still standing where she'd left him. He hadn't stepped in and brushed Sable or moved him into his corral. He was running his hand over Ambrose's head, and her floppy-eared donkey shoved his head through the corral to be touched.

He didn't say a word as she quickly brushed her horse, but he did open the corral gate so she could take Sable in, and he waited for her while she checked their water and gave them each a flake of hay. Then he opened the gate for her, latching it behind her. He glanced to the house and rubbed his head. "I'd like to grab a shower," he said. He didn't finish, but she wondered for a minute if he was going to ask her to come with him. At the same time, she wanted to talk to him about Michael. No matter where they were, they had to be able to talk about the kids.

"I need to get changed, but I can let you go first," she said, and she watched as he nodded.

He reached his hand out and touched her shoulder, her back, and then allowed it to fall away. "Let's go."

She nodded and took a step, then turned to face him. "I'm worried about something, Neil. Will you tell me the truth, no matter what it is or how bad it is, if I ask you?" She waited and wondered what was going through his mind.

He shook his head. "I don't want to see you hurt, but whatever you ask, I will tell you the truth. I won't lie to you. Fair enough?"

She nodded and licked her lips. Her mouth was

suddenly dry. "Can Maria come and take Michael from me now that we're here, back in Mexico?"

Neil didn't say anything for what felt like forever. He just watched her, and he didn't try to touch her or hug her or change the subject or somehow distract her. "I want to tell you no for a lot of reasons. One, she a signed release of parental rights, which is in that black file I showed you. Two, I am Michael's legal father, and it does reflect that on his birth certificate. But honestly, Candy, Maria hasn't honored anything about our agreement. She kept changing things, and I handled it poorly. Would she try? I wouldn't put it past her. Can she simply show up here and take him? I wouldn't let her get out the front door. I'll talk to Ana and Carlos, I'll hire a guard, I'll do anything so you feel Michael is safe."

"Okay," she said. It wasn't okay. She was freaking out inside, but she also realized this was the first time Neil had really leveled with her. "Hire a guard. Please."

Chapter 19

"Have you talked to Neil yet? He's been gone quite a while," Jed said.

Brad was pacing the waiting area. Both Emily and Diana were sitting with Rodney at Becky's side. Both his girls, Katy and Becky, were sitting on their grandfather's lap, as well. Emily and Diana had been taking turns talking to Becky. "Not yet." He reached into his pocket, pulled out his cell phone, and glanced at the screen. No missed calls.

"I still can't believe that idiot brother of ours pulled that. Seriously, what the hell was Neil thinking?" Jed was the youngest, and he had two young kids and a wife Brad knew he'd kill for. As if with new ears, he was hearing Jed say the same things he'd told Neil. He wondered at what point they would all be done talking about it.

"He did it because he didn't think anything through, Jed. Honestly, I can't imagine what I would have done in his position. I know I haven't always made the best decisions." No, he'd screwed up time and again every time Crystal was involved.

Jed stopped and looked at him, frowning. "This goes beyond stupid, though, even for Neil."

"I'm not excusing him, Jed, but Mom is lying in a hospital bed in there and may not make it, and this thing with Neil and Candy … well, they're just going to have to put it aside for now. We all are."

"You're talking about us?"

Brad hadn't heard his brother come in. He slid around in the chair and took in Candy beside Neil, Andy behind them.

"You're right, Brad," Candy said, and she glanced to Neil. "We are putting this aside right now because your mom has to come first." She appeared flustered for a moment as she stared over at Jed. He thought she was blushing, too, as a hint of pink touched her cheeks. "Jed, it's good to see you. Wish it were better circumstances. Is Diana here?"

Jed actually stepped forward and gave Candy an awkward hug. It was one of those ridiculous obligatory "because we're now related" hugs that their mother always insisted on, but Candy and Jed barely knew each other. He could see it in the shyness that overtook Candy. His sister-in-law tucked up into a clamshell any time a situation made her uncomfortable. Maybe that was why Neil was always pulling her along, taking charge of things. He'd seen it time and again, the shock in her expression when he just did things she wouldn't even consider.

"In with Mom," Jed said. "Both she and Emily are filling Mom in on all the news. Dad's in there, too, along with Becky and Katy. Don't know why they insist on talking to Mom and telling her everything when she can't hear." Jed appeared annoyed. "I mean, she needs to rest. They shouldn't … I don't know." Jed took a step sideways and rubbed his head.

"Jed, it's not hurting Mom to hear us. You heard what the doctor said. We don't know what she picks up in this unconscious state, and you know Mom loves hearing about everything going on with the kids and our lives because she's not here with us every day," Brad said. He wondered whether Jed was going to start arguing, but he realized, too, that this was Jed's way of dealing with things that were out of his control. He could be ornery and pigheaded, and Brad could see how trying to hold it together was making him lash out.

Neil actually touched Candy's arm, and she didn't flinch. In fact, she looked to him. He said, "Let's go see Mom." She nodded, and when he reached for her hand, she hesitated a second before taking it and walking with him.

Brad gestured to Andy. "Things better between them?"

Andy glanced over and then took a seat beside Brad, sticking out his long legs. He was wearing black cowboy boots that were worn and scuffed—far from the Andy he knew. He tapped his fingers on the arms of the chair. "I don't know how bad it was before, only what Neil told me. Whatever he said to her …" He gestured to the hall where Candy and Neil had walked. "She's here. They're talking, at least. You know Neil brought over his head of security from the resort?"

"Why's there security? What's going on?" Jed didn't sound happy, and, by the way he snapped, Brad wondered what he was going to have to say to his younger brother to get him to dial it back.

"Candy's worried about that surrogate showing up and trying to take the baby," Andy explained. "It's a precaution, but a smart one. I don't think Neil would have gotten Candy to come otherwise—which brings up the problem of this surrogate."

The way Andy said it, Brad wasn't sure he wanted to hear his cousin's thoughts. He knew all too well what Andy had done for his dad, always cleaning up the trail of women Todd was done with. If anyone knew how to get rid of a woman and send her packing, it was Andy.

"You're not thinking of doing something underhanded, are you?" Jed said. "Because I know you, Andy, and what you're capable of with women … it's not one of your finer qualities." He wouldn't sit down. Instead, he kept pacing in front of Andy.

"This is Neil's call in the end, Jed, and, seriously, if this was your family, are you telling me you'd let some woman come in and turn your happiness upside down?" Andy shook his head and then linked his fingers together in his lap. "This woman has Neil by the nose hairs, and he doesn't even know it. His head is so out of the game here. Look at everything this woman has done. Seriously, he has a lot to worry about, and he's barely holding it together. So are you saying she should get a free pass?"

Whatever this was between Jed and Andy, Brad had a feeling it was personal, from the past they shared with Diana. Maybe they'd never really move beyond it.

"No, she doesn't get a free pass," Brad said to both of them. "Knock it off, Jed. We're all upset about Mom, but you're starting to push everyone. Andy's right, in a way," he added when Jed gave him a look as if he'd lost his mind. "I read the letter. I was there when Candy got it, and I saw what it did to her. This Maria, the surrogate, she wants Neil. She said in the letter that she wants to be a part of the baby's life, and reading between the lines and knowing everything I do about what happened, I'd say Neil has a lot to worry about. After paying her five million, I'm pretty sure Neil doesn't have much left. So, yes, this thing with

Maria needs to end. Who knows the lengths this woman will go to?"

"So what are you saying, Brad, that you're ready to go strong-arm a woman?" Jed swore under his breath.

"What I'm saying is we get her to agree to what she originally agreed to. Whatever it takes, she goes away, and whatever delusion she has of having some happily ever after with my brother and Michael … Andy's right. We need to settle this. This time, Neil will have us to make sure he's not agreeing to something that'll get him into a whole lot more trouble. He's not thinking clearly. This is a business matter, but he's too close to it, and it's the first time I've ever seen him make a mess of something."

Brad had to stop, because it wasn't just Neil. Brad had done it himself with Crystal, and after years of alienation from his family, not once had his brother and family ever said "I told you so." He'd been a complete ass, not speaking to his dad for years. He knew how vicious and manipulative some women could be. "Hey, you know what? I did it, too, with Crystal. You all know how badly I fucked up, and she turned my life upside down. Let's just sit Neil down. We come up with a plan together, okay?" He took in Jed and Andy, and whatever passed between them had Jed gesturing in surrender.

"Fine," Jed said.

"Andy?" Brad asked.

"Yeah, let's do it. Sometimes, we all need someone to watch our backs."

Chapter 20

It was the smell in the hospital that she didn't like. She was shaking as she walked beside Neil to his mom's room in the ICU. She could see the beds, the people, and the curtain drawn on one side of Becky's bed through the glass. She had a respirator in her mouth. Emily was standing, her hand on the bedrail. Diana was in a chair on the other side, and Candy thought she was holding Becky's hand. Rodney was in another chair at the foot of the bed, each of his granddaughters perched on one of his legs, and he was holding them. It was a scene she didn't want to interrupt. There was so much love here for Neil's mom. She didn't realize she had reached for Neil's arm until she felt his hand cover hers. She was standing so close to him outside the room.

It was the first time Neil didn't say anything. At any other time, he would have said, "It's going to be okay" or "Don't worry," but he didn't. What he did do, though, was slide his arm around her, holding her against him.

"Neil, she looks truly awful," she murmured, and she swallowed. Her mother-in-law, who was always so full of life, was lying there, unmoving. For a moment, Candy was scared to go in. "Maybe I should wait out here." There was a shake in her voice.

"What's wrong?" he asked, and he didn't let her go. As angry as she'd been, she was grateful he seemed to know she needed him now and to feel his support, that he was here.

"I never told you when my dad died. It was here in this hospital, and he was hooked up to tubes and wires …" Her throat felt thick as she remembered the booze and pills he'd swallowed and how confused she'd been for so long. Her father had blamed Neil for his financial problems, but Neil hadn't been the one to swallow the pills and chase them with booze, leaving him brain dead, hooked up to machines until the doctors finally pulled the plug. This wasn't the same, but she worried about when the doctor would come and shut everything down on Becky.

He breathed deeply. When she glanced up at him, he was looking straight ahead. "Let's go in," he said. He led her inside, keeping his arm around her.

Emily was the first to see them. "Hi, you came. I was just telling Becky about the kids' school. The presents she sent arrived for everyone. Katy went to her first dance, a Christmas one, and Becky started dancing, too. Trevor's been helping his dad after school on the ranch." She glanced back at Becky, touched her hand, and glanced over at Diana, who scooted back her chair and dried her eyes with a Kleenex. Diana stopped beside Rodney and touched his shoulder and the girls' heads.

"Katy, Becky, let's go," Emily said. "Your dad is going to take us home. Come say goodbye to Grandma."

It was heartbreaking to watch, as both girls cried as they went to the side of the bed, and Emily leaned down and kissed Becky's cheek before leading the girls out.

Candy hung on to Neil, her arm around his waist, squeezing his shirt between her fingers. His hand was on her shoulder, rubbing and holding her as he watched his mother.

"It's good to see you, Candy." Diana touched her arm and glanced around her at Neil. Then she reached out and pressed her hand to Neil's chest and gave him a sad smile. The way she looked at Neil, Candy realized Diana had a soft spot for her husband. Then she left.

Neil moved away from Candy to his mom's side and bent down to kiss her cheek. "Mom, I brought Candy back with me. Michael and Cat are at the estate, and I know they'd love to see you. All the kids want their grandma back. Every one of us would give up all our presents for Christmas … if you'd just come back to us."

Nothing happened with Becky. The respirator was breathing for her. In and out. Her eyes were closed as if she were sleeping, and there wasn't any hint that she was about to wake up. Even her skin appeared translucent, as if she already had one foot on the other side. Candy could feel death in the room. Maybe that was why she shivered again.

"You cold?" Rodney asked her. She hadn't realized he was still there, but apparently he had no intention of leaving, as he watched her now.

"No, I'm good. I'm just …" What could she say to Neil's father, a man she looked up to, who loved his wife so much?

He gestured to the chair where Diana had been sitting. "Come sit down."

She was about to say no, and she touched the blanket covering Becky's legs. Then Neil took his mom's hand between his and held it, glancing back at Candy, not saying a word. What could he say? She was startled by the loss he couldn't hide. She'd never seen her husband shed a tear. He cleared his throat.

"I'm going to step out and grab a coffee. Dad, Candy, do you want something?" he said as he turned away. She knew the last thing her husband would do was fall apart in front of her. He'd never do that, not Neil Friessen, who always kept it together.

"No," Rodney said. When Neil glanced to Candy, she just shook her head.

She stood there for a moment after Neil left, and Rodney was watching her again. Then he glanced back to his wife. It seemed, from where he was sitting, he was watching over her. He was truly the head of this family, and his wife was such a huge part of it.

"Becky and I have been married for forty-four years," Rodney said. "In March, it'll be our forty-fifth anniversary. Becky wanted to have a party this year, and she planned to surprise you all at Christmas with tickets to fly out here, as she wants all you kids to celebrate. She loves having her grandkids around, seeing her sons all married and happy. And, as she said, she's grateful to have daughters-in-law she actually likes." Rodney smiled and then gestured to the chair again. This time, Candy slipped around Rodney and sat down. She rested her hands on the chair arm and glanced at all the white and faded blue and hospital green around her. And at the equipment that was keeping Becky alive.

"I was scared of meeting you and Becky," she said. "I'm still so embarrassed over that first time when you got home after the storm and discovered Ambrose eating Becky's flowers. I was horrified, and ..." She'd behaved like a crazy person, running barefoot and apologizing. She still remembered the shock on Becky's face. "I thought for a while that you and Becky didn't want me to be with Neil, that he could do so much better. I mean, look at him …" She started to say he was smart and brilliant and sexy and the best damn man she'd ever met. It seemed to her there was something about the Friessen men, their strength, their stubbornness. Everything about them was strong minded, strong willed. They knew who they were. "Were you like Neil, Brad, Jed, and Andy?" she said instead. Although every one of them was different, they each had a domineering and protective attitude their wives struggled with. She wondered now what Rodney had been like at their age.

"I was worse," he said. "The one thing I wanted to do was raise my sons to be a better man than me."

She glanced over at Rodney, and by the way he said it and watched his wife, she sensed a struggle and turmoil in all their years together.

"Candy, what you and Neil are going through is just one of many hurdles you're going to have in your marriage." He raised his hand in the air. "Becky, if she was awake now … why, she'd tell you a thing or two. We've all done things we wished we hadn't, some worse than others. We all have something in our past that we can never make right."

She didn't have a clue what he was getting at, but she knew she'd done her share of things, even forging her husband's name on those hospital documents for Cat during that time when Maria was a poison in their life. She still regretted that, and although Neil had bailed her out, he'd made her suffer at the time, letting her think he'd throw her to the wolves. After all, what she'd done was a crime, but did it compare to what he'd done? She lowered her gaze to her fingers, wondering if Rodney knew. When she looked up at her father-in-law, she knew, without a doubt, that Neil wouldn't have shared what she'd done.

He'd been furious, as he had every right to be, but in the end he'd always had her back.

"I guess sometimes you start to wonder if two people who love each other so much but keep hurting each other should be together," she said. "Maybe it's time to admit that we were never meant to be."

"I don't believe that. Becky and I didn't have any easy road, but I really do believe there comes a time when everything we believe is real will be tested. At that time, it feels as if there's no way we'll ever get past that thing, that wrong that was so awful."

What was he getting at? Was he talking about her and Neil, or someone else?

"What you and Neil are going through is challenging." He gazed back at his wife. "Becky and I have over forty years of challenging that makes what you and my son are in look like a cakewalk."

What could be worse than what Neil had done? It was horrible, it was awful. "Yes, but you respect Becky. I've never heard you tell Becky what to do or try to organize her and her life or be as controlling as my husband is. Sometimes I wonder if I'm going to drown, that's how smothering he can be."

"Candy, sometimes we do things that are so bad we pray no one ever finds out." He looked directly at her. "The really bad thing between Becky and me ... it started with my brother."

Chapter 21

Rodney's brother was Andy's father, Todd, a man she'd heard nothing about except for a few comments from her husband. Neil said the man was a snake, and it was amazing that Andy had turned out to be somewhat respectable.

The fact was that Andy had terrified her once. He was handsome in a dark, dangerous way, and she knew he would protect his family at any cost. She'd been in Montana with Neil when Gabriel had gotten sick, and she'd seen how far Andy would go to get his son a bone marrow transplant. He'd moved heaven, hell, and everything in between, but there had been something about the way he did things, the way he talked … She wondered if skating on the dark side of illegal was something he often did.

"Andy's nothing like my brother, in case you're wondering," Rodney said. "Candy, I've seen how you are around everyone. I think we all scared you at one time. Andy is a good man, and I'm proud of how he stuck around for that young girl he married."

Rodney was talking about Laura, who was so young—maybe twenty-two, if that. When Andy married her, she had been barely legal, a single mother living in her car. Candy knew the story, but it was hard to imagine what Laura had endured.

"Todd is what you would call, in my day, a womanizer. That's a polite way of saying the man slept with everything on two legs, and when his son was old enough, Todd had him cleaning up the trail of women left behind. Todd destroyed women. He has no respect for them, and no woman is out of bounds for him. Including his brother's wife."

Candy couldn't look at Becky. Her eyes were glued to Rodney. She hoped he wasn't going where she thought he was.

"I can see you're shocked."

"I don't know what to say. I see how much you love each other. You're so good together."

"That's years and time to become a better person. We both had reasons over the years to call it quits, to walk away. Any judge in the land would have granted a divorce to either of us. I even remember a time her daddy drove out from the Napa Valley to get his daughter, and he was planning on taking Brad, too. She was pregnant with Neil at the time. Once he saw what was going on, he had a man-to-man talk with me and threatened me with the end of his shotgun. He knew I was being unfaithful, although he never came out and said it."

Was he kidding? Cheating wasn't something Candy had ever pictured Neil's father doing. This was definitely not something she wanted to know about.

"It wasn't physical, Candy, but it did mean something. I wanted to sleep with her. There was something about the woman next door that stirred something in me that Becky didn't, and her husband was always gone. We were friends, and every time she called, I'd go running. We'd talk for hours, and I started to look forward to seeing her and hated going home to see my wife. I never saw it as cheating. I saw June as a friend. She was lovely, she was lonely. I was lonely, too, because Becky wasn't giving me what I thought I needed. But I had married her. I had made a vow of love to her, and her father reminded me of that vow. Divorce, in my day and age, didn't happen often, and my family meant everything to me. I wasn't going to lose my sons. I listened to her father, and then Neil was born." Rodney took a deep breath, and it seemed to be so much effort, as if it hurt.

"But you didn't cheat," Candy said. "You worked through it." She wondered how she'd feel if Neil had confided in another woman—but then, in a way, he had.

"Only because I had my wakeup call first." Rodney just watched her for a minute, and she could see he was thinking of something he didn't like thinking of. There was heartache in his expression. "Things were tense between Becky and me for a while. Neil was a year old when I think everything finally came to a head. Brad was running around, getting into everything, and my brother came to visit. The ranch, which is now Brad's, is where Becky and I lived. It was also where my brother and I grew up. I was the oldest, and as the oldest, my father had left it to me. Todd was always mighty choked about that, but he was family, and when he came and stayed with us, it seemed fine at first.

"He would help Becky. I'd come in, and they'd be sitting at the table together, talking, and then she started looking at him the way she once did at me. We hadn't touched or been together as husband and wife for a long time, and the distance between us grew. I didn't go and see

June anymore, and I had told her to stop calling, but that didn't mean I could forget about her. Becky knew. It wasn't something I could hide, and I think at that point we were about as far apart as two married people can get while living under the same roof. My brother stayed for two weeks, and it was the first time I had seen Becky that happy. Then, one day, he left."

Rodney wouldn't look at her, as she could see he had a lump in his throat. Whatever had happened all those years ago, she could see it still affected him.

"I felt so guilty over wanting the woman next door and feeling stuck with Becky because I had married her. It was an obligation, and I had two sons. And then she wasn't happy anymore. I'd come in and find her crying. My brother had been gone for weeks, and she started acting strangely. It was the crying. She tried to hide it. She'd always go off into the bathroom or another room, thinking I didn't know. But I knew, and I thought it was because of me. I never imagined it was because she was pregnant."

"So that was when Jed came along?" She knew the brothers were close in age.

Rodney turned her way. "Becky and I hadn't slept together since before Neil was born."

Holy shit, she couldn't believe what she was hearing. No, no. Not Becky. She was the last person Candy could see as deceitful, as a cheater. "So Jed is …" She couldn't imagine that Jed wasn't Rodney's. Seriously? Then she realized it was worse. It had been Rodney's own brother messing with his wife. That was just horrible.

Rodney was shaking his head. "No, it wasn't Jed." He rubbed his chin, and then the glass door slid open, and Neil reappeared, looking from his dad to Candy.

"Everything all right?" He looked to Candy, and she was wondering what was showing on her face. She was screaming inside. She wanted to know what else had happened. Did Neil know, she wondered?

Rodney cleared his throat and pushed out of the vinyl chair. He looked to Candy and then Neil. "I'm glad to see you two together," he said, and he held her gaze for a minute. "I need to stretch my legs," he added. Then he walked out.

Candy watched the door and then glanced back to Becky, lying in the bed. The respirator was pumping air into a woman she thought she knew, a woman she respected, someone who had it together. She realized there were a lot of things about Becky that no one knew.

Neil ran his hands over his mom's hair and said, "I know this is hard. Mom really liked you. She kicked my ass a time or two and didn't hesitate to let me know when I was overstepping with you. She told me to be a better husband." He smiled down at his mother. "She's an inspiration to me. Her and Dad, the years they've been together, they just figured it all out, you know?"

She couldn't say anything, not with the bomb Rodney had dropped on her. She glanced toward the door, feeling an overwhelming need for air.

"You ready to go?" Neil asked her.

She scooted back her chair and stood at the side of the bed, staring down at Neil's mother, a woman who had been nothing but kind to her, a woman who had cheated on her husband. Without a doubt, Candy realized Rodney had shared a secret with her that no one else in the family knew.

Chapter 22

"Look, Trevor's not going to the hospital, Brad. He's staying here at the house," Emily said. She had been agitated ever since they left the hospital, ever since they'd walked in and found Trevor glued to the TV, watching one movie after another.

"Em, I disagree. I think Trevor can handle this. We took the girls, and they're upset, but it's important. I think they need to say goodbye."

Brad and Emily were in one of the guest rooms in the wing beside his mom and dad's room. Andy and Laura were down the hall, and Jed and Diana were on the other side of the house, where Neil's wing was. This house was huge, and his mother had kept rooms for them so she could have the entire family come and visit at the same time.

Brad kicked off his boots and sat on the edge of the bed, pulling off his socks. Emily was pacing in front of him in her dark jeans and green, striped sleeveless shirt. He knew she was on edge, worried about his mother, about the girls, about Trevor, about everyone. He reached for her arm and pulled her toward him until she was sitting in his lap. He ran his hand down her leg, then up over her hip and her side.

"Brad, he doesn't understand things the same way Katy and Becky do. This will be too hard on him, seeing your mom with a tube in her throat—and the fact that she won't wake up, I don't know how to explain that to him." Emily slid her arm around his neck and leaned her head against him, cheek to cheek.

"He understands a lot more than you think he does. You know that. You've even pointed out to me that he picks up on how everyone is feeling better than we do. He knows something is up, he just doesn't ask a hundred questions like the girls do. You saw him when we got here. Even now, he's agitated, out of sorts. He needs to see her. We'll explain it to him." He was holding her, feeling her against him, wishing over and over that they could be here under any other circumstances. "Trevor asked where the Christmas tree is, where the presents are, you know," he murmured. Brad wondered if Emily had heard. She had to have, because Trevor had asked at least a dozen times, but nobody could come up with a reasonable answer for an autistic child.

"Brad, why is it that Christmas seems to be the one time of year people die. I don't want your mom to die. I want her to wake up, but that isn't realistic, is it?"

He couldn't say a word about losing his mom, because it was killing him inside. Even when he and his dad hadn't spoken for years, his mom had always been there. She was the one who always made everything okay. She was the one who made the Friessens who they were. "We can hope for the best, but I don't know, Emily."

She sighed against him. "I know you're right, I just don't think I have it in me to answer all the questions

Trevor's going to have, Brad. Christmas … he was so looking forward to it this year. It's all he's been talking about, and it's a week away. How can we have Christmas now? This isn't fair for anyone."

It sucked. Brad, who loved Christmas every year, for the first time loathed everything about this day. He couldn't stand the thought of losing his mom, but what was worse was losing her over Christmas. It would devastate all of them, especially the kids. "I know, but we've got to push through, Em, for the kids."

She sat up and linked both her arms around his neck. Her nose brushed his, and she didn't hide any part of herself or how she was feeling from him. She leaned in and pressed her lips to his, and she lingered, running her hand over his cheek. She opened her mouth so he could taste her, and she was sweet and slow. This was his connection with her, his wife, the one woman he truly loved. Then she was pulling at his shirt from where it was tucked in his waistband and yanking it free.

"Em, what are you doing?" he whispered as she turned to him and straddled him, putting both hands on his face and kissing him again, deeper. Feeling the heat and the need in her, he knew she, too, needed this closeness the way he did.

"I need you," she whispered against his lips. "I need to feel you inside me, Brad." She pulled at his shirt again. This time, he pulled it over his head and tossed it. Then he wrapped his arm around her waist and flipped her around on the bed until she was lying beneath him, her legs wrapped around him.

He took charge of kissing her, of tasting her. He needed to feel her around him, listen to her cries when she came with him, and he wasn't interested in taking his time. They each pulled off their clothes, and Brad was on the bed and inside her. When he held himself above his wife, looking down on her, her blue eyes watched him with so much love and emotion, an unspoken commitment. He believed, with everything in him, that there was something about their love and their commitment that was beyond time.

Chapter 23

Candy had been so quiet from the moment they walked out of his mom's room. They'd stopped briefly in the waiting area, where Diana and Jed and Andy were sitting. His dad had been over by the window, looking out.

"Dad, we're going. Did you want to ride back to the house with us? You can get cleaned up, rest a bit, and come back," Neil said.

His dad looked his way, glanced at Candy, and then shook his head. "No, I can't leave. I fear if I do, something will happen. I'm going back in."

For a minute, Neil considered staying, but there was something in Candy's expression that made her look shell shocked. Maybe it was from seeing his mom this way. Of course it was. She had to be upset. They all were.

"I'm going to go and sit with Uncle Rodney," Andy said, leaving the waiting room to head after him.

Diana sat beside Jed and put her hand in his. "We'll stay. Would you mind checking on the boys, see if they're okay?" Diana asked Neil. "Or should I go?" She turned to Jed. "I don't want to leave you here alone."

"Diana, stay with Jed. It's fine. I'll check on your two monsters and see if the house is still standing," Neil said. He was trying to lighten the mood. He loved his nephews, but they were a handful, and they reminded him so much of when he, Brad, and Jed had been young. He knew they had tested everything in their mother. She was a saint for putting up with all their shenanigans. But then, their dad wasn't a pushover, either, and he'd backed up their mom time and again. They were the perfect partners.

"Thank you, Neil," Diana said, and she squeezed Jed's hand. Jed was looking so distracted.

"I'm going back in, too. Diana …" He stood up, and she nodded, taking his hand. They were so in tune with each other.

Neil watched as she leaned on Jed as they walked down the hall. Then he glanced down at Candy, who was standing beside him, her arms crossed. She was distracted, lost, thinking of something. "Are you okay?" He couldn't help reaching out and touching her face, brushing back a strand of dark hair. She didn't flinch this time. He was grateful for that.

"We should go," she said, but she waited for Neil and then started toward the elevator. He pressed the button and waited, and the doors dinged and then opened.

"Oh, Neil, I came as soon as I heard," came the cry from the elevator. Stella Delinsky, his banker friend, was a vibrant seventy-year-old woman with deep red hair, a heavy coating of makeup, and a blue, cap-sleeved dress that fit her like a second skin. She strode out of the elevator on stilettos that clicked on the floor. She had a confidence and a "take-no-crap" attitude he'd never seen in anyone else before, and she had a mouth on her that could make a sailor blush.

She held her arms out and hugged Neil, then reached for Candy and wouldn't let her sneak away. "Honey girl, you have been in my every waking thought since you up and left with this guy. How are you?" Then she waved her hand before they could say another word. "Well, of course you're not okay!" She was a short woman. Even in the four-inch spikes she was wearing, the top of her head didn't pass Neil's shoulders. Even Candy, his tall, long-legged wife, was a head taller than the fiery redhead leading her back to the waiting area.

"Neil, run down to the cafeteria and grab some tea for us," Stella said. Tea, seriously? They had to go.

"Stella, we have kids at home," Neil called out after her, and Candy glanced back at him with a helpless look.

"Tea, Neil, now. Go. Tea makes everything better!" She was out of earshot now, and Candy glanced his way again. This time, she shrugged and gestured for him to go.

<hr>

THE PROBLEM with Stella was that she was a woman with a strong mind. There wasn't a man around who could pull anything over on her. She directed Candy to a chair and sat down beside her, crossing her short legs. The slim skirt rode over her aging knees. For the life of her, Candy could never figure out how Stella managed to walk around in shoes that high. She knew without absolute certainty she'd break her neck if she tried, as there was no way to balance in them, but Stella made it look easy. Perhaps she had been born in them.

"Tell me everything. How are you?" Stella had vibrant blue eyes, brought out by the smoky shadow outlining them. She reached for Candy's hand and patted it between hers. "Candy, I've known you a long time, and I've watched from the sidelines while you and Neil have struggled with so many things. When you finally got married, it did my heart proud, because I'd said for a long time, 'Stella, those two are meant for each other.' You fought it, and it took a damn storm to rip through here and take out that ramshackle dwelling you lived in to bring you together." Stella wasn't one to beat around the bush.

"Stella, you're Neil's banker. You carried the loan on my land that my dad left and the bank took from me. You know a lot of secrets that you carry for everyone, so I think you already know things are at a crossroads with Neil and me."

"Yes, I do," she said, watching Candy closely.

"We have two kids. Cat we adopted from the orphanage. And Michael is a baby Neil bought from a surrogate. Oh, and it's his. He lied about it to me." She was tired of talking about it, and the way it came out sounded worse than it was. Stella pursed her lips and gave Candy one of her looks as if she was ready to give her a talking to.

"Candy, there's one thing I know better than anyone. When a man does what yours did for you, that's love. Twisted, fucked-up, but he loves you." Candy looked around, because Stella could be a little loud, and, in the hospital, her colorful language could get them kicked out. "You worry too much, Candy. You always have. Your dad lied to you, too, but you always cut that damn drunk slack. Made excuses for him, too."

"What?" She couldn't believe this. What the hell did her dad have to do with any of this?

"Your dad wasn't the saint you make him out to be," Stella said. "We've talked about this before. He kept you from Neil, told you how Neil was after the beachfront property for his resort, and that you were his means to get it. And you believed him. Did you know Randy went to Neil and Rodney demanding a partnership, a corner office, and his name attached to the Friessens'? When your husband wouldn't go along with it, your father said he would make sure you had nothing to do with Neil ever, that you would hate him, and your father sure made good on his promise, didn't he?"

She had never heard that part. She had realized when Neil rescued her that her father had been wrong, but that he had actually lied to keep her away from the one man she longed to be with? Well, it hurt. It couldn't be true, though. "Neil told you that?" she asked, wondering why he would say such a thing.

"No, I heard it from Rodney."

Candy didn't know what to make of that. Why would Rodney tell Stella something like that? She glanced out to the hall, and Stella patted her hand.

"I'm not a fool, Candy. Something like that, you know me well enough to know I don't take anyone's word for anything. I went to the horse's mouth and talked to your dad before he downed all those pills and drank himself to death. He laughed about it and said even after he was gone, he'd make sure Neil never got his hands on anything of his."

Hearing that her only parent, whom she loved more than anything, could do something so horrible, for such selfish reasons, deepened the ache in her heart. "Neil never said a word about it. Why wouldn't he tell me?" Her voice cracked.

"Tell you what?"

She looked up at her husband as tears stung her eyes. He was in front of her, holding two steaming paper cups.

"Stella just told me about what my dad did," she

replied, and she watched Neil and the heavy, hard look he leveled at Stella.

"Oh," he said.

Any other person would have been trying to smooth things over with her husband, but not Stella. "Now, you listen to me, Neil Friessen. She needs to hear what that no-good drunk did. You've got a hell of a mess here, and, for the first time ever, seeing you two together … well, damn; I don't want anything to come between you two and mess up this happily ever after. You know, some of us never had that, and mine is seeing you two together and finally believing that not every man out there is completely worthless.

"Now, Neil, Randy was a total dirty dog. Candy, he may have loved you in his own worthless way, but your dad always put you second to what was good for himself. Candy, he lied to you about Neil, and you believed him. Neil, you always were the better man, but when you paid five million dollars to that young, foolish woman … Yes, I saw the bank draft. At first I thought to myself, 'What kind of trouble has Neil gotten himself into?' Then I dug and had Harry, our investigator, do some digging, too. I couldn't believe it! Neil Friessen digging himself into one big pile of caca."

Neil handed Stella one of the paper cups. Then he reached for a chair and turned it to face Candy as he sat down. He held out the other cup to her, and she could see the vulnerability in him. She took the hot, steaming cup, and it burned her hand. Neil must have noticed, as he took it from her and set it on the ground under his chair.

"Neil, why didn't you ever tell me what my dad did?" she asked. Why was he so insistent on keeping things from her?

"He was your dad, Candy. No matter what he did, I

know you loved him. What would be the point of taking away whatever illusion you were holding on to that he cared for you? He's dead now, and I won't apologize for not saying something. I didn't want you to know. It was awful, and it was hurtful. It wasn't okay, what he did. I can see, looking at you now, how it's messing with you."

"Why would my dad lie?" She was stunned. Of all the hurtful things that had happened between her and Neil, he'd never have sold her out like Randy apparently had.

"I don't know, honey, but dads are supposed to love you and protect you. Randy didn't, and if he was alive now, I'd probably kill him with my bare hands for doing what he did." Neil took her hand between his and held it. She didn't pull away from his touch. There was something about being here with him and all this ugliness, the secrets that were coming out from everyone, that had her holding on to him.

"I don't want to be lied to anymore," she said. "I want the truth, no matter how much you think it's going to hurt me. I love you, Neil, but you've hurt me so badly."

He reached out and brushed his fingers over her hair, tucking it behind her ears. "No more secrets, okay? The truth. We talk, we work it out."

She held his gaze. It was deep and meaningful, and she knew he meant what he was saying.

"Well, we should start with one of the biggest problems you have, Neil Friessen," Stella interjected. "You have no money left in your account. Your resort has an operating line of credit that's maxed out, you have employees who need to be paid, and you gave what was left of your money away to a woman who carried your baby and——"

"And is now trying to turn his life upside down," Andy said, walking toward them. He took in Stella, her appearance, and there was a flash of amusement there. Candy would bet anything Andy had never met anyone quite like Stella.

"Is this true, Neil?" Stella snapped. She was so direct and sharp, cutting through bullshit better than any man Candy had ever met.

Neil was watching Candy as he spoke to Stella. "I moved my family as far away from Maria as I could. She found me, and she sent a letter that my wife opened." Neil shook his head. "I almost think she did it to hurt Candy. She wants to see the baby. She said she wants to be part of his life. I screwed up, Stella." He took a breath. "I screwed up big time." He said it again to Candy as he held her hand, his legs surrounding hers. "God, help me, please! Get her out of our life."

Andy put his hand on Neil's shoulder, and Stella patted his knee.

"Well, seriously, I think it's time this young lady understands what it means to honor an agreement," Stella said. She stood up, picking up the clutch purse on the chair beside her. "All right, Candy, you need to forgive Neil. Neil, you fuck up again, I'll kick your ass." Then her face softened a bit. "And I'm so sorry about your mother. Please tell your father my thoughts are with him and your family."

Candy didn't miss the frown on Andy's face.

"She's awake!" Jed yelled from the hallway. Neil was up, and Candy followed, touching his arm. "Mom opened her eyes!"

Neil turned around and pulled Candy into his arms, hugging her so tight. She could feel his relief, and she could feel the tears he was trying to hide from everyone. She put her arms around his neck and held the back of his head, just staying there with her husband.

Chapter 24

"It's not going to fit, I told you!"

Jed was arguing with Brad over the Christmas tree they were dragging into the house. It was massive, and it looked as if they'd cut it down from somewhere on the grounds. Candy actually had to look closer at the blue spruce, because she was sure it was from the gardens in back that Becky had planted. She had said she missed the trees from home, and pines and spruce had been flown in. Candy saw the expression on Neil's face where he stood, holding Michael in the crook of his arm, and then his gaze went across the room to Candy, and he shook his head and smiled.

He stepped closer to her, then leaned down and kissed her again. "I love you," he said, and she couldn't help but reach up and touch his face.

"I know," she whispered back, and he slipped his arm around her, pressing closer to her. "Is that one of your mom's trees?" she asked, though she already knew the answer. She watched Brad, Andy, and Jed putting it up in front of the bay window in the front room. They were arguing, discussing, strategizing, and they cheered when they stood it up with an inch clearance to the high ceiling.

"Pretty sure it is. Mom's going to be mighty pissed if it's the one I think it is."

"I can take the baby if you want to get in there," Candy said, watching the kids, all excited, bouncing in front of the tree with boxes of ornaments and decorations ready. Cat stood with Trevor, and it was Andy who leaned down and lifted her so she could hang a decoration on one of the taller branches.

"Hey, everyone! I have hot chocolate," Emily called out, carrying a tray in.

"Em, it's like eighty degrees out. How about lemonade instead?" Brad said. It was hot, but thankfully the house was air conditioned.

"Brad, when you decorate a Christmas tree, it calls for hot chocolate," Emily said, putting down the tray. The kids all hurried over, calling out for some.

"With whipping cream and shortbread cookies," Diana called as she carried another tray, Christopher hanging on to her leg. Laura followed, carrying Jeremy, and Katy was right behind her, holding Chelsea.

"You know, I think they've got it," Neil replied. "I can't think of any other place I'd rather be right now."

She pressed her head against him, and he kissed her forehead.

It had been five days since Becky opened her eyes and the doctor removed her ventilator. She'd suffered a massive stroke, and her speech was slurred and her right side was paralyzed, but she was alive. She had since been moved to a private room, and Rodney was still with her. Next week, she would be moved to rehab, and a nurse was being hired to stay with her.

"Are you okay with us staying here in Mexico for a

while until Mom's on her feet?" Neil asked again, like he had several times this past week.

"Yes, I am. You never told me what happened yesterday when you met with Maria. When you came back with Brad and Jed and Andy, I don't think I've ever seen them so quiet."

"Well, I don't think my brothers or cousin have ever had dealings with a woman quite like Stella, let alone let her run the show."

Candy turned in his arms and took in her smiling, content baby, who was taking in the massive tree three grown men were arranging in the living room.

"Stella took charge," Neil explained. "Gotta love her, she cut through the crap with Maria. You know, when we showed up at her house, this big new house she bought, she wasn't the Maria we met. She was older, dressed for business, with a makeover to go with it. She was waiting in her office for us. It was startling, the change. I'm very glad now that Stella was in charge and that Brad, Jed, and Andy were beside me. But it was worth it to see the look on their faces when Stella informed them of the do's and don'ts of the meeting. She didn't let any of them say a word. I'm telling you, I'm glad she's our friend. Even Andy said he'd never want to go up against the likes of her."

"So what did she say to Maria, Neil?"

"She made it clear she could no longer live here in Cancun. She'd worn out her welcome, and that her money was tied up in Stella's bank, a Mexican bank, by Mexican laws. If she expected to be able to have access to the wealth of money I paid her, she would cease any and all contact with me, with you, and with Michael. She signed an agreement stating that if she violates any of the terms of the agreement, she'll lose every cent I paid her."

"How can Stella do that?"

"The money is in a trust now, and it's controlled by Stella. She did that for you, honey, for me. She said it was the only way to get Maria to move on. Sometimes, when someone's heart is breaking, the only way they can move on is if someone makes them."

She was watching, wondering if there was something more he wasn't saying.

"I'm telling you everything, but I also know, from Stella, that there are things in Maria's past that have made her who she is, just like all of us. Here, I wanted to give you this." He stepped back and pulled a folded paper from his pocket.

"What's this?" It was thick and white, and when she opened it, she wondered if she'd start crying.

"It's the adoption. It was couriered this morning. It's final."

She blinked back the tears as she looked up at Neil.

"Michael is officially ours. Yours and mine. Merry Christmas, baby," he said, and she reached up and put her hands on his face and kissed him.

"Hey, you two, this is G-rated down here," Jed called out, and Andy whistled.

"What's G-rated, Dad?" Trevor asked, and everyone started laughing.

"I'm glad you came," Rodney said.

Becky was in a wheelchair, dressed in light blue slacks and a striped, blue T-shirt. She had a lovely room in the care center, and Rodney was standing behind her, pushing her into the middle of the room. Becky mumbled something.

"What's that, dear?" Rodney leaned down, and he seemed to understand what she was saying or was trying to say. He patted her hand. "I'll tell her."

Every time Candy walked into the room where Becky was, she remembered something Brad had said. They didn't have cheaters in the family. It stung to realize she knew something that Neil, Brad, and Jed didn't.

"Candy, sit down, honey. Becky wants me to finish the story," Rodney said.

She looked over at Rodney, and she didn't miss his exchange with Becky, who looked up at him and nodded. "She heard what you said?" Candy asked. She pulled up another chair and sat across from Becky, and Rodney pulled over another chair and sat beside his wife, taking her good hand in his.

"Yes. I'm not sure she heard it all, but enough. She wants you to know everything. You have to know, my wife, she was gorgeous. This blond girl stole my heart with the brightest eyes I'd ever seen, and I was a handsome rogue and I knew it. The passion we had, I thought it would never go away. But that heat and chemistry burned out before we were even a year into our marriage, and when we drifted like we did … well, you know what happened. It was one of those moments you never forget, hearing how she was carrying another man's child."

Candy was watching Becky holding Rodney's hand. A tear slid down her wrinkled cheek. She had aged so much since her stroke that she appeared older than Rodney.

Rodney cleared his throat. "I lost it. It was a dark period of my life, of our life. I yelled and I screamed and raged, and she cowered in a corner, terrified of me. I was so close to hitting her, beating her. I actually understood that moment when a man snaps. I stepped back, and I grabbed my shotgun, and then Becky was there, screaming, pulling on my arm because she was afraid of what I was going to do. I started for the door, and she knew I was going to hunt my brother down and shoot him. She held on and screamed, and then Brad was there, crying and watching, this little kid in saggy diapers. I could hear Neil screaming from somewhere in the house, too, but I was going out that door and I was going to kill my brother. I even grabbed an extra box of shells from the cabinet at the back door.

"I went out the door, and Becky was holding on, digging her feet in the dirt, trying to slow me down. I reached my truck, and I shook her off until she fell in the dirt, and I climbed into my truck and drove away, watching as she raced after me, crying, and then dropped to her knees." Rodney stopped talking and took in the sadness in Becky's expression. There was a shared pain between them that Candy couldn't imagine.

"We were so young when we got married. I was so arrogant when my dad died and I was given the ranch. We didn't have any guidance from anyone close by. We were just trying to figure things out, and when you're young, it often comes with so much foolish pride and anger. You say things that, years later, you wish you could take back."

"Well, what happened?" Candy asked. "You obviously didn't kill your brother, as he's still around."

"No, I didn't, because the sheriff stopped me five miles from home. Becky called and told them what I planned to do, which probably saved both our lives. The sheriff threw me in a cell until I cooled off, and about eight hours of sitting in a cage has a way of sobering a man up to whatever stupid notion is going through his mind. So, I'm in my truck, going home with every intention of ending my marriage. When I walked in the front door, I could see Brad sitting there in the living room with a bowl of cereal. Neil was lying in a playpen in the living room, kicking his legs up in the air, and then ..." He stopped and looked over at Becky, and his breath caught as if he was having trouble finishing. Becky turned her one hand over, her arm resting on the edge of the chair. Candy looked at it, and Rodney rested his hand over one of her scars, rubbing his hand over it.

"My wife was standing in the middle of the room, her face tear stained, blood covering her arms. She had tried to kill herself. Her legs gave out by the time I reached her, and I lifted her and carried her into the bathroom. I grabbed towels and tried to stop the bleeding, but she'd lost so much blood. I have never in my life been so terrified."

Candy couldn't believe this couple had done any of these horrible things. She was having trouble seeing Rodney as the man he was describing, and Becky was a strong, confident woman, the mother of the three most capable, strong-minded, men she'd ever met! It just didn't sit right with her. Maybe the shock of hearing all of this showed on her face.

"I told you the story"—Rodney stopped and looked at Becky before he could continue—"because if there are people who were ever meant to be together, it's you and Neil, and Brad and Emily, and Jed and Diana. Becky and I watched from the sidelines as you and Neil destroyed your relationship and your love for each other. Neil has never loved a woman the way he loves you, and whether you know it or not, Candy girl, you are good for him. You're growing, becoming stronger, more confident, and it's a pleasure to see."

"So what happened with the baby?" Candy said. She needed to know what the turning point was that had made Rodney and Becky the couple they were today. They were so close, and they loved each other. She was sure they were each other's best friends. But how could any couple get past what they'd done to each other?

"I got Becky to the hospital, but she'd lost so much blood she miscarried. She spent a week in the psych ward, and her mom and dad came up and stayed with us when she got out. They stayed until they knew she was going to be okay, that we were going to be okay. Her father took me aside and told me there was something about Becky that had made me so crazy as to marry her, and he made me sit down with him and take passion out of the equation, looking at the qualities that had drawn me to her. He said I needed to come up with at least a half dozen qualities about Becky that I loved, or he was packing his daughter up with his grandkids and taking them back to California. We'd get divorced, go on our separate ways.

"I realized he was serious. I had to think, because when you first meet someone, it's that connection, that chemistry, that zing that draws you to them. The last thing you're thinking of is compatibility. But her dad was dead serious. Thank God we came up with more than six, because even with how bad it was between me and Becky, I knew I didn't want to lose my family. And we worked at it, Candy. We started talking every night, every morning. Me and Becky, we talked. In between raising Brad and Neil, she'd help me on the ranch. She learned to drive a tractor, and that was mighty impressive. She learned to ride a horse, and if she was scared of something, she'd take a deep breath and dive in. Then Jed came along. When he was three, she surprised me for our anniversary and renewed our wedding vows. Every year after that, on our anniversary, Becky and I would steal out into the moonlight and remind ourselves of our love for each other, and every year, just the two of us alone, we renew our vows."

Becky was smiling, one side of her face drooping as she reached up with a shaky hand and touched Rodney's face.

"This year, for our anniversary, we made a promise. All you kids are going to be here when we renew our vows."

Turn the page for a sneak peek of
THE REUNION the next book in The FRIESSENS
Available in print, eBook and Audiobook

**The family you thought you knew.
A reunion you'll never forget.
A love that lasts forever.**

Join the Friessen siblings, their spouses, and kids as they gather to celebrate their parents' wedding anniversary. Amidst the joyous occasion, long-buried issues resurface, testing their love and trust in each other. As tears are shed and old bonds are strengthened, an unexpected twist arises – cattle rustling gone wrong! Get ready for a wild and unforgettable reunion, where anything can happen when this family comes together.

—"I love love love these Friessen men. To have a love so deep and pure for their women is awesome. They show the true meaning of family and togetherness."

KINDLE CUSTOMER

—"This is a tight knit family, along with their cousin Andy, his wife and their children. The kind of family we all wish we had."

SUSAN

The Reunion

This wasn't home.

After a moment, when she allowed the confusion to clear, she understood this was where she lived now. It was her new home. She'd survived a stroke, but even through her days of hell, balancing on the edge of leaving this world, she'd never once considered not fighting her way back. She'd lost faith only once in her life, and never again would she believe that taking the easy way out was actually easier. Some days were harder than others, but she pushed on. She couldn't give up.

She'd done that once. That had been a time in her life when she was young and foolish, believing everything she wanted was something she couldn't have. She had always been looking for something better, not understanding that what she already had was all she needed. It was right in front of her, but then, at times she hadn't been able to see it. She had been making choices in fear, acting as if she knew everything. She soon discovered, as the years went by, that she knew nothing at all.

There was a lot to be said for age and wisdom, for

living through every heartbreak imaginable—many of her own making. She hoped she was a better person, all her choices having brought her to this one moment in time. She was Becky Ann Friessen, Rodney's wife, mother to Brad, Neil, and Jed and their wives, Emily, Candy, and Diana. She was a grandmother, a friend.

A breeze picked up, whistling as it stirred the waves over the salty ocean. Becky could hear them pounding the white sandy shore. She could smell the salt in the air, and she breathed again until it settled her. She wanted to go down to the water, to walk there herself and wade into and through the waves as they slapped against her legs, soaking her linen pants. But she wasn't there yet. Almost, she told herself. She believed it as she stared at the cane resting against the light oak nightstand beside the bed, beside the easy chair she was sitting in.

Her skin was damp even with the breeze blowing in. It was warm again, like every other day in Cancun, the home she and Rodney had retired to. She was in the perfect chair before the open window, staring out at the vibrant colors from the gardens below: the reds, greens, oranges, and pinks. Her roses, orchids, and lilies were all in full bloom, and it was in moments like this, when she caught a scent from her garden, that she would remember the young girl who fell in love, had her heart broken, and then pulled a knife across her wrists, allowing the blood to flow out of her just to make the agony stop.

She stared at the white lines now, faded from forty years ago. The memory too had faded over the years—what she had done, what her husband had done. Something happened when you stood between life and death that reminded you of everything you'd forgotten. Becky tried to forget and blank it out as she moved through life, becoming stronger, more confident, and finally feeling as if she was worthy of her husband's love.

She took a breath to clear her head and took in the warm tones of her room, the white trim, and the floor-to-ceiling windows in the pocket doors that could transform the bedroom into a veranda on a whim. This was new, and her son Neil had taken it upon himself to change this bedroom into a paradise while Becky was recovering from her stroke in the rehab center. It was comfortable and nice —and because it was Neil's idea, as always, it was over the top.

She took in the ivy green sectional, the ottoman, and the large flat screen mounted to the wall. She had teased Rodney that their large bed was made for a king, but to her, Rodney was a king, not just for who he was but because he had stayed with her and worked on their marriage, loving her for her.

Rodney wasn't a saint. He was rough around the edges, and he'd made his share of mistakes, her tall, dark-haired, devastatingly handsome man. At times in his younger days, she'd teased him about what a stick in the mud he could be, so set in his ways. He was cocky, arrogant, confident, and there hadn't been a woman around who didn't try to get his attention. He was the son of a wealthy rancher, a senator, a rodeo star. He had been everything to her, as only a young girl with starry eyes could see him.

Rodney had always known what he wanted. Anyone who paid attention could see that. It was in his walk, the way he took in what was going on around him and everyone he was with. He was brilliant. Even at such a young age, as a young man of nineteen, he had known there was more to people than what they said. She didn't know that at the time, but then, everything she'd learned now from her years of struggles allowed her to see how truly special her husband was.

Rodney was the eldest Friessen son. He was a hard worker who made a success out of everything he did: the cattle ranching, his time in the rodeo. He had set eyes on Becky for the first time when they went to the same school, Berkley. She'd heard he was in the rodeo, and she remembered their first date, when she had tagged along with him to the rodeo grounds. He'd ended up facedown in the dirt, scrambling to get out from under a bucking bronco after making his time. He had been amazing.

She remembered it as if it were yesterday. The blueness of his eyes had made her heart skip a beat in her slender chest. Her throat had squeezed at something in his expression that she couldn't put her finger on. His powerful eyes had been set on her. Maybe that was what had made women from everywhere want him. She sure as hell had. He was heart stopping, the best-looking man she'd ever seen, with a body she had wanted to step closer to. The way he moved, his slim hips and long legs ... even his deep red checked shirt hadn't been able to hide his chest and shoulders. Rodney Friessen had grabbed her attention.

She'd been sitting on a worn bench, wearing a yellow sundress, watching him. A white sunhat perched on her head, her waist-length hair flowing in soft waves. He glanced her way, then looked once, twice, three times. There was no mistaking it: He'd noticed her. Then he had dug in with each step and walked towards her. It had been a moment in time she'd never forget, burned into her memories. That had been their first date—and the moment she realized she had to have Rodney, that he was the one.

"There you are," her husband's deep voice called out

behind her. "Your nurse is downstairs, ready to go for the day. Are you sure you don't need her to stay?"

She had to blink as her memories flashed from a young, dashing Rodney to her tall, older husband. She swore the man was even more handsome today than he'd been forty-five years earlier. How was it possible for a man to have aged better than a woman? His eyes softened as he stepped closer, resting his large hands on his hips, his gold band flashing on his finger. Then he touched her where she sat in the easy chair, another of Neil's new additions.

Rodney didn't pull away, instead running his large hand over her shoulder and leaning down to kiss her cheek. She pressed her hand over his, maybe to hold him there. She loved his touch and didn't want him to walk away.

"I'm good," she said. The words were coming easier, not as slurred and unclear, but then, she'd fought an aging body and a debilitating stroke that had left her with paralysis on one side. Her mind had remained clear, but she was stuck in a body that didn't want to work. It had been so hard in the beginning, because in her mind, she was still that young, beautiful girl who had stolen Rodney Friessen's heart. Only when she caught a glimpse of the old woman in the mirror staring back at her did the icy reality crash in.

"You sure? This is your first day home." He was worried. She could see it in his expression even though they'd both wanted this for so long.

She patted his hand again and then forced herself to slip to the edge of the chair and push herself up. She reached for the cane as she stood, willing her body to move as she once had. Rodney, of course, didn't let her go but instead held on to her, helping her stand up.

"Don't look so worried. I'm stronger than you think," she said. This was the man she'd married, and she couldn't imagine spending another moment away from him. At the same time, she didn't want him playing nursemaid to her —to see her as useless, frail, and weak. "I wouldn't be home if I couldn't look after myself. You know that. Now why don't you take me downstairs so I can talk to my son about his need to redo our bedroom?"

"You don't like it?" He was still holding on to her, and she loved his touch as a husband, not as a man worried she couldn't keep herself together. "I wanted you to have a space you're comfortable in. I wasn't sure …"

What was he going to say? Was he expecting the nurse he hired to sit up here all day with her? She hoped not. Although she liked Nola, she needed to look after herself. She had struggled to bathe and dress herself for weeks, and she'd be dammed if anyone would treat her like a child incapable of tending to her personal needs. It was degrading, that's what it was. She wouldn't have come home if that were the case. Maybe Rodney needed to understand that.

"Rodney, my love." She reached up and patted his cheek, taking in her wrinkled hand and the dull gold band still on her finger, the same one she'd worn for almost forty-five years from the day Rodney had slipped it on her finger. She didn't think she could get it off now even if she wanted to. "Stop worrying so much. I'm home, and I don't need Nola hovering over me as if I'm going to fall at any moment. This change …" She took in the newly renovated bedroom and the sheer curtains that fluttered when a breeze swept in. "It's lovely. Now let's go."

When she slipped her hand on his arm, he gave her a look as if he didn't quite believe her, but at least this time he started walking with her to the door. His hand latched over hers to hold her to him.

"So tell me, when are all my children arriving?" she

asked. They made it to the top of the stairs, and she focused on the circular stone steps. At one time, she'd loved the deep orange tile, but going up and down these stairs now was better than an aerobics workout at the nearest gym.

"Surprise!"

She nearly dropped her cane at the chorus of voices, looking down into the open foyer where her grown boys, their wives, and her seven grandkids were waiting. "You're here already! Oh, this is wonderful."

One, two, three—she counted them again: Brad, Jed, and Neil with Cat sitting on his shoulders. Her daughter-in-laws, Emily, Diana, and Candy, stood with their husbands, each with an eye on their children, her grandkids. There was something about each one of them, something in their tired, distracted expressions, that Becky recognized all too well. Each woman was holding on to something.

"Lorhainne Eckhart is one of my go to authors when I want a guaranteed good book. So many twists and turns, but also so much love and such a strong sense of family."

(LORA W., REVIEWER)

Amidst a joyous parental anniversary celebration, the Friessen siblings and their families reunite, only to confront buried conflicts, strain their love and trust, shed tears, rekindle bonds, and face an unforeseen challenge – cattle rustling gone awry – in a wildly unforgettable family gathering.

"Lorhainne Eckhart has this uncanny way of just hitting the spot every time with her books."

(CAROLINE L., REVIEWER)

The O'Connells: *The O'Connells of Livingston, Montana are not your typical family. A riveting collection of stories surrounding the ups and downs of what goes on within a family but also with some suspense, angst and of course a bit of romance thrown in for good measure. "I thought I loved the Friessens, but I absolutely adore the O'Connell's. Each and every book has different genres of stories, but the one thing in common is how she is able to wrap it around the family, which is the heart of each story." (C. Logue)*

The Friessens: *An emotional big family romance series, the Friessen family siblings find their relationships tested, lay their hearts on the line, and discover lasting love! "Lorhainne Eckhart is one of my go to authors when I want a guaranteed good book. So many twists and turns, but also so much love and such a strong sense of family." (Lora W., Reviewer)*

The Parker Sisters: *The Parker Sisters are a close-knit family, and like any other family they have their ups and downs. Eckhart has crafted another intense family drama… "The character development is outstanding, and the emotional investment is high…" (Aherman, Reviewer)*

The McCabe Brothers: *Join the five McCabe siblings on their journeys to the dark and dangerous side of love! An intense, exhilarating collection of romantic thrillers you won't want to miss. — "Eckhart has a new series that is definitely worth the read. The queen of the family saga started this series with a spin-off of her wildly successful Friessen series." From a Readers' Favorite award—winning author and "queen of the family saga" (Aherman)*

Billy Jo McCabe Mystery: *The social worker and the cop, an unlikely couple drawn together on a small, secluded Pacific Northwest island where nothing is as it seems. Protecting the innocent comes at a cost, and what seems to be a sleepy, quiet town is anything but.*

Lorhainne loves to hear from her readers! You can connect with me at:
www.LorhainneEckhart.com
lorhainneeckhart.le@gmail.com

Also by Lorhainne Eckhart

The Outsider Series
The Forgotten Child
A Baby and a Wedding *(An Outsider Series Short)*
Fallen Hero
The Awakening
Secrets
Runaway
Overdue *(An Outsider Series Short)*
The Unexpected Storm
The Wedding

The Friessens: A New Beginning
The Deadline
The Price to Love
A Different Kind of Love
A Vow of Love, A Friessen Family Christmas

The Friessens
The Reunion
The Bloodline
The Promise
The Business Plan
The Decision
First Love
Family First
Leave the Light On
In the Moment
In the Family
In the Silence

In the Charm
Unexpected Consequences
It Was Always You
The First Time I Saw You
Welcome to My Arms
Welcome to Boston
I'll Always Love You
Ground Rules
A Reason to Breathe
You Are My Everything
Anything For You
The Homecoming
Stay Away From My Daughter
The Bad Boy
A Place of Our Own
The Visitor
All About Devon
Long Past Dawn
How to Heal a Heart
Keep Me In Your Heart

The O'Connells
The Neighbor
The Third Call
The Secret Husband
The Quiet Day
The Commitment
The Missing Father
The Hometown Hero
Justice
The Family Secret
The Fallen O'Connell
The Return of the O'Connells
And The She Was Gone

The Stalker
The O'Connell Family Christmas
The Girl Next Door
Broken Promises
The Gatekeeper
The Hunted

The McCabe Brothers

Don't Stop Me (Vic)
Don't Catch Me (Chase)
Don't Run From Me (Aaron)
Don't Hide From Me (Luc)
Don't Leave Me (Claudia)
Out of Time

A Billy Jo McCabe Mystery

Nothing As it Seems
Hiding in Plain Sight
The Cold Case
The Trap
Above the Law
The Stranger at the Door
The Children
The Last Stand
The Charity
The Sacrifice

The Street Fighter

Finding Home
Finding Honor

The Wilde Brothers

The One (Joe and Margaret)
The Honeymoon, A Wilde Brothers Short

Friendly Fire (Logan and Julia)
Not Quite Married, A Wilde Brothers Short
A Matter of Trust (Ben and Carrie)
The Reckoning, A Wilde Brothers Christmas
Traded (Jake)
Unforgiven (Samuel)
The Holiday Bride

Married in Montana

His Promise
Love's Promise
A Promise of Forever

The Parker Sisters

Thrill of the Chase
The Dating Game
Play Hard to Get
What We Can't Have
Go Your Own Way
A June Wedding

Kate & Walker

One Night
Edge of Night
Last Night

Walk the Right Road Series

The Choice
Lost and Found
Merkaba
Bounty
Blown Away: The Final Chapter
He Came Back

The Saved Series
Saved
Vanished
Captured

Single Titles
Loving Christine